Piper

Piper

Meg Harper

USBORNE

In memory of
Rose Shepherd (1959–2006)
Nick Bishop (1955–2007)

First published in the UK in 2007 by Usborne Publishing Ltd.,
Usborne House, 83-85 Saffron Hill, London EC1N 8RT, England. www.usborne.com

Copyright © Meg Harper, 2007

The right of Meg Harper to be identified as the author of this work
has been asserted by her in accordance with the
Copyright, Designs and Patents Act, 1988.

The name Usborne and the devices ♀ ⊕ are Trade Marks of
Usborne Publishing Ltd.

A CIP catalogue record for this book is available from
the British Library

JFMAMJJA OND/07   9780746073131   Printed in Great Britain.

1

I don't know where I am. Beneath me, the ground is damp and hard, prodding me with pebbles. I open my eyes gingerly and quickly shut them again, the morning light too bright and terrifying. I have been here all night then; that's why my body is so stiff and cold. I don't want to move. I can bear the pain in my head and my hips if I lie still; I am numb with the chill of the night. But once I so much as stretch a toe, I know that I will be in agony. And somehow, I have to get home.

I shift my weight to my hands, readying myself for the push to sitting. One, two, three, push. And here it comes.

Pain – shattering, sickening, heart-stopping pain. My ever-present companion. So then. At least I know that I am alive.

Tanith tried to settle the little rucksack more comfortably on her shoulders, then took it off and repacked it yet again. It was a delaying tactic, she knew. She didn't want to go but she had no choice. She had to leave the tiny two-roomed cottage that had been her home for fourteen years before anyone discovered that her grandmother had died and that she had been left alone in the world. It had been no surprise when her grandmother had agreed.

"You must leave here, Tanith," she had said, every breath an effort. "If you don't the Cratz will find you."

The Cratz. The aristocrats, the autocrats, the bureaucrats. The ruthless wealthy who clung to the top of this deeply divided society and would do anything to stay there. Tanith shuddered at the thought of a life enslaved by them.

"I know," she said, gripping her grandmother's hand tighter. "Don't worry. I'll go."

Her grandmother's frail fingers returned the pressure.

"Tanith," she whispered. "There's something I should have done long ago and never did. Something very important. I want you to do it for me."

For a moment, Tanith wondered if her grandmother had finally lost her senses but her eyes were as clear and sane as ever, holding Tanith's in an irresistible gaze.

"There isn't much time left, Tanith," she whispered. "No,

don't cry. You must be strong and brave. Stronger and braver than I have ever been. Listen – listen carefully."

Tanith clutched her grandmother's hand in both of hers, tears still oozing down her face. They dripped unheeded off her chin onto the muzzle of the wolfhound who lay, blanket-like, around her huddled body, a continuous low whine in his throat. The moment Tanith had dreaded for so long had come.

"We should get help," she sobbed. "You should let me get some help."

Her grandmother shook her head, little more than a quiver. "No, Tanith," she said gently. "I want to die here, in this bed, with just you by my side. You alone have cared for me these last months – why should I need anyone else? But first you must hear my story. Now stop wasting my breath and listen."

Tanith daren't delay any longer. The first fingers of dawn light were beginning to spread themselves across the night sky. She needed to be away long before Mr. Haltwhistle, the farmer who had let them squat in exchange for their help on his farm, realized that anything was wrong. There was a letter for him which Tanith left propped up on the rickety table.

Like any other Citz, Tanith and her grandmother had been forced to scratch out a living in whatever way they could, working for Mr. Haltwhistle and coaxing puny misshapen vegetables out of the thin, polluted soil around their cottage. Tanith had grown tough and hardy but she was short and her limbs were stunted. She was often racked with pain in her hips and knees. Now that it had come, the thought of leaving the shelter of the cottage was grim. A long, cold trek would be torture.

Worse still, she had to leave her beloved grandmother tucked neatly into the bed they had shared, her hair brushed, her eyes closed peacefully, the sheet pulled up high. She couldn't bear to cover the old lady's face. It was too final. Too hopeless. As it was, she could at least wave goodbye from the doorway. She could blow a kiss and imagine one blown back.

"I'm off now, Grandma," Tanith whispered, choking on her tears. "I'll do what you asked, I promise. You take care now." Then she clicked her fingers to Wulfie and shut the door carefully. The moon was still up, making the frost-crusted grass glisten. It would be all right. Even if Mr. Haltwhistle didn't come by for a couple of days, Grandma would be fine, cold but undisturbed, safe in her chilly tomb.

Tanith knew where she was going. It wasn't a good place but, burdened with her grandmother's task and terrified of being picked up by the Cratz, she hadn't much choice. She was going where scores of other kids ended up – the nearest city. There she would soon be invisible – just another scabby orphan trying to survive. It was about twenty kilometres away so ought to be manageable in a day but Tanith would have to travel in the dark. She was scared of being noticed with her strange waddling gait. And then there was Wulfie, of course. There was no question of leaving him behind. Apart from the fact that he would have wakened the whole valley with his howling, Tanith loved him almost as much as she had loved her grandmother. And he would be warmth and protection. Not that she had much confidence that he would defend her – he was trained to kill rabbits, not people – but he was big and shaggy and looked fearsome. He had been an effective deterrent at the cottage.

Now, instead of loping ahead, as he usually did when they were out on the hills, Wulfie remained glued to Tanith's side. There was barely room for them to walk together on the path. Every so often, he whined.

"I know, Wulfie, I know," whispered Tanith, blinking back tears. "This is awful. But it could be worse. The Cratz could get us. And then we'd be split up, no question."

Resolutely, Tanith plodded on. She was tired. Sleep had been scant for the last few days and she ached from her vigil, cramped up on the bed with her grandmother, not wanting to leave her for a moment. She had forced herself to eat before they left but knew she would have to rest soon. Her aim was to reach an outcrop of rocks, high on the gritstone ridge which glowered over the city. She and Wulfie could worm their way into a cranny and sleep throughout the day. She had often run and hidden there when other kids chased her and called her names. Later, when darkness fell, she and Wulfie could start the long trek down towards the city. She must ignore the nagging pain in her hips, master her nasty, chilling fear and swallow the lumpy grief that hurt her throat. Right now, they must carry on trekking upwards to the gnarled stump of a Celtic cross which stood on the horizon, a solid, gritty reminder of stories most people had forgotten.

Tanith paused for a moment to catch her breath. There was no danger of her forgetting her grandmother's story. It had cut deep into her heart and would remain there for as long as it took to solve its horrific riddle.

2

Crow pulled off his battered denim jacket and the layers underneath it, then tied up his slick, black, chin-length hair with a broken shoelace. He bowed to his audience. His face was long and lean. With the hair pulled back, the height of his cheekbones was obvious. Despite his grimy skin and ragbag clothes, he had an exotic look, his eyelashes so dark and short that he'd been accused of darkening them with charcoal. He was bone-thin, but wiry and he managed to make his paint-stained, torn, close-fitting jeans look like something from a Cratz catwalk.

There were appreciative gasps from the girls in the audience as he picked up one of the firestaffs which lay on the floor and lit the wick ends from his makeshift brazier.

Then he started his show. Once alight, the firestaff whizzed from one hand to the other in a dizzying figure of eight. People shuffled backwards, excited but slightly alarmed now. The firestaff circled Crow's neck, dived beneath his legs, flipped under one knee, then the other. Suddenly he was lighting a second staff and the crowd pulled back still further, gasping its admiration and fear. It was impossible to tell which end of the staff was which, where one ended and the other began. Crow was a white-chested, whirling stick-man silhouetted in a nimbus of roaring fire. Money was raining into the hat that he had put out. Crow was grim-faced with concentration but inside he was smiling.

His eyes, his nerves, his muscles were completely focused on the dancing staffs but his ears were still alert for the sound of any threat. He had not survived on the streets of the city without discovering the instincts of the wild animal. He knew what he had heard in the distance. Police sirens. And coming his way. Unlicensed busking was an offence; he'd been warned often enough. And there were no licences for fire. But it drew in the crowds and was as honest a money-spinner as anything else. It angered Crow that the police bothered with him. What would they have him do? Drugs? Robbery? Darker deeds that he didn't want to think about? He listened, foxlike, assessing the proximity of the threat. Money was still flying but if the police came any nearer, he would run. Fire was his provider and protector; he couldn't afford to lose it.

Crow darted into the sandstone tunnel and hugged the damp, crumbling wall. He fought to get control of his breathing so that he could listen and check. No, no one was following him. He never took chances though. You didn't hesitate; you just ran. There was no time to waste. All he ever stopped for was to hide his bucket – the one he filled with water from the river in case of accident – which was cumbersome and noisy. The firestaffs he slung across his back and the money went straight in his body belt. He would only stay here in the caves and tunnels which burrowed into the sandy rock that bounded the city's greasy river for long enough to be sure that there was absolutely no threat of pursuit. The police rarely pursued anyone this far. Only kids lived in here; only kids dared to and then only out of desperation. The caves were said to have been inhabited during prehistoric times; the network of tunnels had been dug out during the world war a hundred years ago, for the city people to hide from German bombers. But other stories abounded, rumours to make you quake. So most people avoided them and the police, charged with rounding up street kids but hard-pressed and short-staffed, left well alone. Kids on the streets they occasionally dealt with; to the kids in the sandstone they turned a blind eye.

But Crow wouldn't live there; he had a horror of caves and tunnels for reasons of his own. His squat was the bottom of a long-abandoned mill, a few kilometres upstream, which he guarded fiercely from other squatters with his fire and any missiles he could find. It wasn't ideal. Though overgrown and with no access any more, the steep riverbank that rose above it bounded a Cratz country park. He dreaded being discovered by some interfering rich Cratz walking a dog. He couldn't attack them with fire and wood – if he did the police would want him for more than unlicensed busking. But he'd been all right so far, mostly sleeping in the day. Though he caught fish from the river in the early morning, he never cooked it there, waiting to do that in the city at night. He couldn't risk being given away by the smoke of a fire and the smell of cooking. Only the police seemed to care about the number of kids on the streets of the city; for everyone else they had become part of the landscape, like litter. But in the suburbs and the village enclaves where the Cratz all lived – that was something else. Crow would be as welcome in the country park as a heap of steaming dog turds.

Just as Crow was about to head out of the tunnel to retrieve his bucket – the night was young, it was worth finding another pitch and giving another show – he heard panting and a kid blundered into him.

"Uh!" gasped the kid, winded by the impact. He'd been running hard. "Who's that?"

Crow didn't think twice but grabbed the boy by the

neck, spun him round and locked his arm across his chest. With his free hand, he flicked his lighter to examine his prisoner. The boy's eyes rolled back in his head, trying to see who had captured him.

"Crow?" he squeaked and Crow felt the child relax against him.

Crow shook his head and let the boy loose. He didn't question how the kid knew who he was. He was well-known in the city. "Stupid," he said. "You've got to be quieter – and watch where you're going. You won't survive long if you carry on like that."

"Yes, Crow, sorry, Crow," said the boy, still breathing hard.

"Don't apologize," said Crow, harshly. "It's you, you should say sorry to. You could have got yourself killed. Supposing I'd been someone dangerous? Or supposing I'd thought I was being attacked? Don't you know the risks? Kids in the city – they go missing all the time, and no one even notices. You were very lucky."

"I know, Crow – but I haven't been here long. It's hard." There was a sob in the boy's voice that he was fighting to suppress. Crow looked him up and down in the light of his flame, assessing whether he was telling the truth. Yes, the boy still looked soft.

"Parents dead?" Crow asked, more gently.

The boy nodded. "My mum, anyway," he said. "My dad went off ages ago, when she got sick. He was frightened he'd get it, I think."

"I'm sorry," said Crow.

"She was ill a long time," said the boy, his voice breaking. "I thought she might be one of the ones who got better."

"You'd best come with me," said Crow, his voice gruff. "I can show you a thing or two that'll help."

The boy hesitated, trying to gulp back his tears.

"You know who I am," said Crow. "It's up to you whether you trust me."

"I'll trust you," the boy sniffed.

"Good decision," said Crow. "What's your name?"

"Timbo."

"Right, Timbo. Follow me."

3

I am so hungry. The pain in my belly is worse than the ache in my hips and knees. That is dull and throbbing, something to live alongside, something to get used to. This is sharp, an attack on my guts, making me double over. There was soup today, if you could call it soup. Mother said it was spinach but I'd like to know where she got spinach from. It was nettle, no mistake. Oh fine and good for us, I'm sure, but not filling. As filling as stagnant, weed-choked pond water. It might as well have been; it looked much the same.

I can hear them talking, muttering away. They think I'm

asleep. Talk, talk, talk. Why do they waste their precious energy, talking deep into the night? Trying to find a solution? There is no solution but one – and I wish it would come quickly.

Tanith awoke deathly cold. Wulfie had shifted a little in his sleep and there was a gap between their bodies where the chill had crept in. She snuggled closer, wrapping her arms around him, pulling her legs up into the crook of his haunches, the hunger pangs in her stomach soothed by the weight of his warmth. She ought to get up, she knew. The light was beginning to fade and she wanted to make it to the city that night. She guessed they had neared the outskirts now although they were still hidden in the valley. They had been following the river down from the moors, struggling to find their way in the dark, wary of slipping into the water but not daring to climb up to find a road. They had walked for two nights and slept for two days, Tanith very strict with the meagre rations she had packed, Wulfie fending for himself as usual. It would be good to reach the city tonight though; Tanith would need more food soon and to make some sort of base for herself and Wulfie. She didn't know how; she didn't know where. All she knew was that scores of other kids survived somehow. Loads didn't – but she wasn't going to think about that. She had Wulfie and she had Grandma's secret. She would survive; she had to.

She would make a start now. Deep in this river valley, steep, sandy, overgrown banks rising to one side and spoiled land stretching across to a grimy blur of housing on the other, she didn't think she would meet anyone. And if she did, the sight of Wulfie looming in the twilight ought to be enough to scare anyone away. Ever since the hard winters had begun, there had been talk of wolves in wild places.

Tanith scrambled awkwardly to her feet. Two nights sleeping in the open had done her joints no good, despite huddling against Wulfie. She was stiff and her hips hurt, especially the one which had taken her weight. Her knees weren't too bad though. That was a relief. Maybe the walking had been good for them.

"Come on, Wulfie, let's go," said Tanith and immediately he was up, panting by her side. He had barely left her since they had set out, apart from to hunt. She patted his rough, brindled back and he turned his big head, his anxious eyes questioning.

"It's all right, Wulfie," said Tanith, smiling. "Don't look so worried. I'm just being friendly."

Then she picked up her backpack and they set off.

It was almost dark when Wulfie suddenly stopped stock-still in the middle of the path, his head up, his nose twitching, so that Tanith almost fell headlong.

"Wulfie, don't do that!" she gasped but he had gone, scrambling up into the bushes to her left, careless of anything but dinner. Tanith walked on slowly, stumbling a bit. On this overgrown track it was easier with Wulfie beside her. His huge chest forged a way through, forcing down brambles, ferns, nettles – with his rough fur, he didn't care. And he gave her stability, something to grab when she lost her balance. He would be back soon, she was sure, invigorated from gorging on some furry snack. She wished it was as easy to feed herself. Wulfie could bring an animal down for her, she knew, but then there would be all the business of skinning and cooking and she didn't have time for that. She wanted to be lost from view in the city as soon as possible. There had been no sign of pursuit but the spectre of some grasping Cratz, keen to enslave a respectable young Citz, still haunted her. She quickened her pace.

Just then, Tanith heard a sharp, loud yelp, up in the bushes to the left. Wulfie! She'd recognize his yelp anywhere. It came again, frantic, frightened. Then, instead of the crash and brush of him charging back to her... silence.

"Wulfie!" Tanith cried and then bit her lip. Whatever, whoever had hurt him, she shouldn't give herself away if she could help it. She paused, undecided, and then, her heart lurching, she started scrambling up the steep bank, careless of the noise she was making, hanging on to roots, hauling herself up any way she could, digging her toes into the sandy surface, desperate to find her dog.

Despite the pain in her joints, she climbed quickly. She was tough and strong and had rested all day. In any case, she was fuelled by horror and anger. If someone had hurt Wulfie, her friend and protector, they would pay. She would kill them if she had to. She didn't know how but she would.

She paused, her arm wrapped around a slender tree trunk, her feet jammed into the slithering earth.

"Wulfie, where are you?" she said, a catch in her voice. Her resolution was beginning to falter. She was near to giving way to weepy panic. She peered into the gathering gloom. It was impossible. How could she find a grey, hurt dog in the twilight unless he barked? She took a risk.

"Wulfie!" she shouted, cupping her hands round her mouth. "Wulfie!"

Then she heard it, a whine, a whimper, the scrabbling of his big paws. And not far away. Maybe he was stuck in a hole. Maybe he had fallen and was lying injured somewhere. Immediately, Tanith was off again, oblivious to any danger to herself, slithering awkwardly back down the bank for, this time, Wulfie's voice had come from beneath her, closer to the river.

The woodland loomed darker now or so it seemed. She thought she must be almost back on the track but further along. Yes, there was the river, glinting in the twilight. Tanith sat down, shoved off and slid or shuffled the last stretch down to the path. She picked herself up, noting in alarm how much better trodden the earth was here, rounded the corner and came to an abrupt halt.

There was someone blocking the way, someone holding what appeared to be a huge lighted brand.

"Get back," the someone snarled. "Get back or I'll use this."

Tanith stepped back quickly. She had no doubt that the tall lad she could now see lurking behind the flame meant what he said. But she had no intention of abandoning Wulfie.

"I'm looking for my dog. He ran off hunting and I think he's hurt. Is this Cratz land? Are you a Cratz?"

It was a challenge. Of course it wasn't Cratz land. No Cratz would dare go near a wild place like this. They preferred to stay safely in their village enclaves. And of course he wasn't a Cratz. His ragtag clothing told her that. So what right had he to threaten her with his fire and his words?

"So it's your dog," said the boy, unmoving. "He was after my fish."

Tanith almost laughed. Stupid old Wulfie. He loved fish but had never managed to catch any for himself. These would have been easy pickings, hanging temptingly from the boy's belt, glistening in the moonlight. But Wulfie hadn't managed to steal them.

"Where is he now?" she said, trying to keep the tremble out of her voice. "You'd better not have hurt him."

"You should have kept him under control. What are you doing here, anyway? How did you get down here?"

The boy was staring at Tanith in a way she didn't like, his gaze uncannily bright in the gloom. Unaccountably, Tanith shivered.

"Why should I tell you?" Tanith demanded. "Show me where my dog is."

It was a gamble. The flaming brand was terrifyingly near her face. And she believed this boy had hurt Wulfie. Why shouldn't he just finish her off and take what little she had? No one would ever find her, deep in this wood. But he hadn't attacked her yet. Why not? If he was some sort of bandit, what was there to stop him? *So*, she told herself, *he doesn't really want to hurt me because he hasn't hurt me yet.*

"I've tied the dog up," said the boy. "He's not badly injured – just terrified. I might have singed his fur a bit."

"Show me where he is!" Tanith insisted. "He isn't yours and this land isn't yours. Show me where my dog is, you thief!"

"I'll bring him," said the boy. "Stay here."

But Tanith was too eager. As the boy turned to go, she stumbled after him, suddenly tearful but determined to get to Wulfie as soon as she could.

The boy rounded on her. "I said, stay here!" he snarled and once again, the brand was in her face.

Tanith blenched, gazing up into the dark, elvish eyes which glimmered behind the flame. And suddenly, her aching body didn't want to go any further. Her limbs felt warm, her head was woozy. All she wanted to do was stay still and wait.

I must be tired out from the walking, she thought. *Yes, I am. I'm very, very tired.* Without another word, she sat down in the path and the boy left her. But the moment he had gone, the wooziness eased too. Tanith leaped to her feet, alarmed and suspicious. She should have followed the boy – this might be a ruse to make his getaway with Wulfie. What a moment to have felt faint!

Suddenly there was a frantic barking and Wulfie came storming through the undergrowth, followed by the boy. Tanith was almost knocked over, such was Wulfie's excitement. The boy steadied her, holding her elbow while she shouted at Wulfie to calm down.

"Why didn't you bark for me, Wulfie?" Tanith exclaimed, wrapping her arms around his neck. "I didn't know where to look!"

"Fish," said the boy, looking at her strangely. He sounded puzzled. "I let him have a bit. I thought he might be my friend."

Tanith hugged Wulfie fiercely. "No," she said. "Never. He's *my* dog."

The boy nodded. "I see that now. But take my advice. Keep him close. A big dog like that – there's a lot of meat on him."

Tanith gasped, horrified. "But surely no one would... I mean, he's protection, he keeps you warm, he's..."

"It depends how hungry you are," said the boy. "But there are other reasons that people want dogs. Lots."

"Thanks," said Tanith, stumbling away from him. She still felt a touch light-headed. "I'd better go now... I..."

The boy raised a hand in farewell. He held his flaming

brand like a torch now, as if he would light her way. "Take care," he said.

Crow waited till Tanith was out of sight before scrambling back to the mill to pack his kit for a night on the streets. She was an odd one for sure. Very odd. She hadn't liked him, understandably perhaps. He, on the other hand, had been drawn to her. Her feistiness, her devotion to her dog, her clear, bright eyes, passionately defying him. Defiance. He wasn't used to that, especially from girls. It was unsettling – exciting. He had noted her strange, waddling walk. He wondered how long she'd survive. And how long she would keep her dog.

4

By the time Crow reached the tunnels, night had fallen. Despite the darkness, his arrival had been noted. From a couple of arches dug into the rock face, pale faces emerged.

"Crow! Crow's here!" voices called, and within a few moments a score or so of skinny, ragged kids came skittering out to besiege the boy.

"Tell us a story, Crow! Show us some tricks! Have you got anything for us, Crow?"

Crow smiled but wearily and squatted down by a small fire which smouldered in front of a bigger cave.

"Fish," he said. "Help me gut and cook these fish and you can have some."

Immediately, an excited babble broke out and scrawny hands tried to snatch at the limp river trout which dangled from his firestaff.

"Patience!" snapped Crow and swung the staff in a swift, wide arc, almost knocking some children flying and causing others to jump back in alarm. "Wait your turn – there's enough for a little each – just wait!"

An uncanny hush settled on the children as Crow's eyes swept the small crowd. As if it was second nature, they formed a quiet, orderly queue and Crow doled out fish, one puny trout to three children.

"No scrapping," he said. "And see that you share fairly."

Then, having checked that they were all busy with their assortment of broken knives and makeshift skewers, Crow turned his attention somewhat grumpily to the fire. Smoked fish was tasty but the children were undoubtedly ravenous; he needed to cook quickly, he needed more flame.

A tall, angular girl who could have been a model in a different life, approached him. She had long, dark curls, tied back with a grubby crimson bandana.

"What's bitten you then, Crow?" she said. "Barely a smile for your troupe today?"

Crow pulled a rueful face. "Sometimes I get weary of it," he said. "You know that, Asta. It's not like I ask them to cling to me. Sometimes I'd just like to be free."

"And what would happen to them then, Crow? What would have happened to me?"

Crow stood up and stepped away from the fire which was now burning well. Immediately, the children clustered round, their fish slivered and skewered on the points of their sticks.

"I met a girl in the woods by the river today. A girl our age," said Crow, ignoring Asta's question. "There was something wrong with her – the way she walked, it was odd – jerky and awkward. She had a dog with her – huge, a wolfhound."

"She was coming to the city?"

"Of course. Everyone knows the streets are paved with gold." Crow laughed, cheerlessly.

"Everyone knows it's a place to hide," said Asta. "Did she say what had happened to her?"

Crow shook his head. "I didn't ask. She was very angry with me."

"Angry? With you?"

Crow shrugged. "She had a right to be. She thought I was trying to take her dog."

"Were you?"

"I would have done if he'd been alone. In fact, he took some of my fish. There'd have been more for the kids, but for him."

"So? What's really bugging you? She's just another kid. Sink or swim. Hide or die. Why so glum about this one?"

"I dunno. She just got to me somehow. She was tough –

there was no doubt about that. Hard to win over. But she was frail too. That walk. And she really needed that dog."

"That's not good."

"I'm going to look for her." It was a snap decision. Crow had been fretting about the girl ever since she had left him in the woods, his thoughts continually returning to her, jabbing away like his tongue at an ulcer.

"Crow!" exclaimed Asta. "She's just one more kid! You could be days looking for her! And why her? The ones that need you, find you. You don't have to go looking for them!"

"This one I do." Crow's narrow jaw was set. It was the way the girl had looked at him, clear-eyed, defying him. It wasn't all about her need; it was about his. He *wanted* to find her.

"Crow! Kids are dying in these streets all the time. What's one more? Oh, I know that sounds dreadful – I know it could have been me – it could be any of us. But it doesn't make sense to pick one out just because you're a bit more sorry for her than the others."

"Look, Asta, I met her," said Crow, choosing his words carefully. "I know about her. We talked. I can't just ignore that. She's disabled and she's with a big dog. So she's vulnerable, noticeable and has got something a lot of people want. I have to try and find her – before it's too late. You could help me, Asta."

Asta shook her head. "Who's going to be here for this bunch while you're off on your wild goose hunt? And what makes you think we want a crippled kid here? The dog, maybe – now that's worth looking for."

Crow scowled. Asta wasn't usually so harsh. But then he didn't usually go looking for waifs. As she said, they found him quite readily enough. He wondered if she suspected that he hadn't told the entire truth about his reasons for searching. Well, it was tough. She would have to live with it. And with the girl, once he found her.

5

I am playing by myself in the yard, hurling my hard wooden ball against the outhouse wall, trying and trying again to force my awkward limbs to move quickly enough so that I can catch it. It bounds away from me, always in a different direction, always unpredictable, the wall is so rough. Sometimes I can do it; there is nothing wrong with my eyes and my hands can easily match the pace, though my arms are short. It gets easier as my body warms.

And then, a wild one. Up, up it flies, way beyond my reach and then down. It lands right in the middle of the stinking midden. It is my only ball. Though it is poorly shaped, one that a passing pedlar let me have out of pity and because he couldn't sell it, I have to get it back.

The midden is foul – rotting ends of vegetables, chicken muck and dead leaves, soft and treacherous. It has stolen my ball. I prod with a branch where I think it fell and yes, there it is, deep inside but within my reach. I lean in. My hand closes round the hard, slimy sphere and I think of eyeballs. The next moment I scream and let go. The pain is excruciating and I want to pull my hand away but I cannot lose my ball. I grope around, gritting my teeth against the gunk and the queasy feeling in my stomach. But the other's teeth find me again. This time I hold fast but I cannot keep quiet. I am screaming, shrieking, bellowing in pain and my mother is running from the cottage with a broom and is beating, bashing, thrashing at the midden and the thing which is living inside. The stench and the pain overcome me and I am gagging, fighting for my breath and for clean air.

Tanith woke to hands round her throat and nothing but someone's foul breath to breathe. She could hear Wulfie barking frantically.

"Finish her, can't you?" shouted a man's harsh voice. "I need your help with this beast!"

Eyes bulging, Tanith just caught the blur of Wulfie, flailing at his attacker, barking and snarling. The fact that he hadn't been killed already gave Tanith an almost supernatural burst of energy. Her assailant had mistaken her stunted limbs for weakness and had thought his job nearly done. She dug her sharp, broken nails into his hands, wrenching them aside and kicking hard into his groin; he was completely taken by surprise. In the time he took to recover, Tanith scrambled up and was away.

"Leave, Wulfie!" she shrieked and instantly Wulfie abandoned his attacker and was running by her side. The man, however, was not to be dissuaded. He had been wrestling hard with the huge, grey beast, desperately trying to land a blow with his cosh that would stun not kill. Now he was wired up and frustrated. He wasn't about to give in, even if his partner had been brought down by the vicious little runt who was making off as fast as she could. What hope did she have, the loser? He would get her in seconds – and her dog.

He reached out and caught her rucksack easily, swinging her round so that he towered above her and could grab her shoulders in a fierce, iron-clamp grip.

She spat in his face. "If you try to kill me," she blagged, "my dog will kill you first. And I will help him."

As if to prove her words, the dog was suddenly upon him again, huge paws on his shoulders.

"Call him off or I'll strangle you!" the man gasped.

"Just try it," said Tanith, wriggling and twisting and bucking in his grasp. "Help!" she screamed. "Someone help me!"

The dog's weight was overwhelming. They all crumpled to the floor – girl, man, dog.

"Help!" screamed Tanith again. "Please someone! Please help me!"

"Keep your mouth shut!" snarled the man. "If you cooperate, I might not have to kill you after all."

Tanith wanted nothing to do with this repulsive, stinking man or his partner who had finally staggered to his feet. She continued to fight, shoving and kicking and wrestling, a pinned fly, desperately trying to get off its back. But she was tiring and knew that she and Wulfie were no match for two big men, armed with clubs. She didn't know what they wanted with Wulfie – clearly they had no use for her – but at least they hadn't killed him. Maybe she ought to listen to what they said. Although every fibre of her being still cried out to fight, she forced herself to go limp.

"That's better," said the man. "Seeing sense at last. Now get this dog off me."

"Wulfie, leave," said Tanith.

Released, the man stood up, hauling Tanith to her feet as well.

"Now then," he said. "You just listen to me. You've got guts, that's for sure. Never seen a runt like you fight so hard. Just come to the city, ain't you?"

"Might have done," said Tanith. The man was wasting his efforts trying to be friendly; he wasn't going to win her over after what he'd just tried to do.

"Let's call that a 'yes'," said the man. "I certainly ain't

seen you before. You or your dog. You're quite a striking couple, even in a city stuffed with unwanted kids. So believe me, that dog ain't going to last long. If we don't get him, someone else will – and at least we ain't going to eat him."

"What do you want him for then?" said Tanith, trying to play cold and hard.

The men exchanged glances. "Hunting," said the one from whom she had escaped.

"Yeah," the other man agreed. "And if you let him hunt with us, then we'll give you some of what we catch. There now. That's a good deal, you know. That means you won't starve in this godforsaken hole. Many a kid would give anything for that."

"What can you hunt round here?" said Tanith, spreading her hands to indicate the disused warehouse she had been holed up in and the broken city landscape stretching out into the distance.

"Whatever's hanging around waiting to be caught," said her attacker. "You'd be surprised what we can catch. But a dog would make it a lot easier. What d'you say now? Is it a deal?"

Tanith had her hand on Wulfie's back. She could feel, rather than hear, the steady growl deep in his chest. He didn't like these men – neither did she – but she didn't have many options. What if she said "no"? Surely they'd just try to kill her and she didn't think she had the energy to stave off another attack.

"He only does what I say," said Tanith, stalling. If she did eventually refuse their offer, maybe the knowledge that Wulfie was useless without her might stay their hands.

"Then you must teach him to obey us too. Or it's no deal."

Tanith swallowed hard. She couldn't bear the thought of letting Wulfie go off hunting with these awful men; she was his mistress and she hugged that knowledge to her with a jealous rage. He was all she had in the world. She would agree to go with these men now but that was just to gain thinking time. Somehow, she and Wulfie must get away from them – and the sooner the better.

6

Crow had been searching and asking all night. At first he had been cautious, asking kids who he knew were loyal to him, kids whom he'd helped when they first came to the city and who continued to survive using the skills he had taught them. He had to be careful. Broadcasting the fact that a disabled girl with an enormous dog had recently arrived in the city would only make her more vulnerable. As the night wore on, however, he took more chances. The longer she was out there, the more she was at risk. Word travelled like hellfire in the city underworld. He could think of scores of people who, once they heard about the girl and her dog, would be moving in to find her – if she hadn't been found already. Why hadn't he done more when he had met her? Why had he been so slow to realize how special she was? He cursed himself for being an idiot. He should have explained the dangers more clearly. If necessary, he should have forced her to stay with him. He'd been too shocked, first by the dog and then by the girl herself. Girls usually took to him. He didn't have a comforting, safe look – that wasn't it. He looked rangy and hard – he suited his name. Girls seemed to like that. This girl hadn't – and it had thrown him completely. His usual resources had failed him and he wasn't used to having to try; it hadn't occurred to him to offer supper or an escort to the city. Fool! It was hardly surprising that she hadn't warmed to him, was it? When she'd first met him, he'd been brandishing a blazing staff in her face and she thought he had hurt her dog! But he knew that wasn't the whole story and it intrigued him.

By the small hours, he was asking kids who'd moved on – kids who he thought still had some loyalty to him but had chosen more lucrative paths than managing on the basic survival skills he had shared with them. They were part of a deeper, darker underworld than his and he was gambling perilously now. It only needed one of these kids to grass to his or her boss and some very nasty characters indeed would be on the girl's tail – if they weren't already. Maybe that was why he had heard nothing; he had expected something to get back to him by now, if only a rumour.

As dawn broke, Crow had to admit that he had got nowhere. And he had nothing in his pockets either. It would be a bleak day for the sandstone gang if he went back penniless. And Asta would be furious. The deal was that they were both there for the kids – on and off, at least. Crow insisted that he couldn't live in the tunnels so Asta bore the brunt of anything that happened there. In exchange, she expected her own earnings to be heavily supplemented by Crow. The system worked well. Asta was a mean spinner of fire poi, the weighted bags which she lit and whirled in dizzying patterns of flame about her head, and she spent odd hours braiding hair in the marketplace. But it was Crow, with his firestaffs and his fire-breathing, his tumbling and his juggling, who was the bigger earner of the pair.

His bony shoulders crooked with anxiety, Crow made his way to the station approach where the well-heeled Cratz were already streaming into the city to work. He nodded at the lad selling *The Even Bigger Issue* even though he despised him for selling something the Cratz had a hand in. What good was a charity magazine in a society as deeply divided as this one? All it did was momentarily salve the guilt of the few conscience-stricken Cratz who hurriedly chucked a few coins in a hat. Then they scurried away to the safety of their policed workplaces or their heavily guarded enclaves in the leafier parts of the despoiled countryside. The sight of the seller's mangy dog, securely tied to a lamp post, reminded Crow painfully of the wolfhound. Even a scrawny cur like this one had hungry eyes watching its every move. If its owner turned his back for a moment, the dog would be gone, off to be someone's dinner. But he didn't think the girl's big dog was destined for the cooking pot. And that was what really worried him.

Quickly, he took up his stance, just at the entrance to the tunnel that led to the platforms. He had space, he was visible and he wasn't in anyone's way. With luck, he could work the pitch for a good hour. He took out his five juggling balls and began. The Cratz would keep their distance but some would throw him their change. He guessed it helped them sleep easier at night.

Forty minutes later, the police moved him on. He didn't bother to argue; he just melted into the crowd as quickly as he could before the cops changed their minds and decided to haul him in. He was tired, cold, hungry and worried. He didn't expect a glorious welcome from Asta – more likely a blistering verbal attack – but when she'd calmed down, she might let him have some porridge and he could kip for an hour or so before he continued his search.

As predicted, Asta was unimpressed to see him and sneered at his earnings.

"A wasted night then," she said. "I told you not to bother looking. I hope that's the end of this nonsense. Even supposing you find this girl, no one's going to welcome her with open arms if the search means we starve in the meanwhile!"

"You won't starve," said Crow, his lip curling scornfully. "You're overreacting."

"*I'm* overreacting?" gasped Asta. "You spend all night looking for this girl that you met for about two minutes and *I'm* overreacting? What did she *do* to you? And don't think you're getting any porridge. With the coppers you've earned, we're going to need everything in that pot ourselves. Go and catch a fish, if you're hungry! Or a dog!"

Crow's cheeks flushed angrily. He expected a little more respect from Asta. If it hadn't been for him, pulling her from the canal three years ago, she'd have drowned or been poisoned by the foul water. She'd fallen, faint with hunger and raging flu. He'd dragged rather than nursed her back to health and taught her most of what she needed to know to survive. All right, so she'd learned to spin poi and to braid by herself but she'd barely known how to gut a fish when he'd found her.

She'd turned away furiously but he grabbed her by the shoulder and spun her round. There was a horrified intake of breath from the clutch of children who'd emerged from the tunnels, disturbed by the raised voices.

For a moment their eyes locked angrily and then all the fight left Asta. Her body seemed to go loose in Crow's grasp.

"I'm sorry, Crow," she said. "That was mean. You always give us whatever you've got. I'm sure we can spare some porridge."

Crow shook his head, blinked and looked away. His face

was tense and unhappy. Asta had a right to be critical and his reaction shamed him.

"I have to go," he said. "I'll find something to eat, don't worry. You're right. The kids need the food."

A small child was tugging at Crow's belt. She looked up at him with beseeching, troubled eyes.

"Don't shout at Asta, Crow," she begged. "It frightens me. Play us a tune, Crow. Make it better."

Crow tried to smile down at her. It embarrassed him to have behaved badly. How could he explain how drawn he felt to the strange, tough girl who was out there somewhere, so vulnerable and conspicuous with her dog, and so totally impervious to him? How could he explain how desperate he was to find her – the one girl in this godforsaken hole who hadn't reacted in the way he was used to, hadn't wilted under his gaze, almost begging to do his bidding? She had stood up to him and had battled for her dog, her wits unclouded. He had to find her. A craving had invaded his soul. She was the one person he had met since his arrival in the city who had eyed him as an equal.

It was hopeless. He couldn't explain it to Asta or anyone else but he could at least spare a moment to soothe the anxious pack of ragamuffins now gathered nervously by the fire. He owed them that.

He felt inside his waistband and pulled out a slim, leather pouch, no more than his hand's breadth in length. From inside, he slid out a tiny wooden whistle, beautifully turned and polished, dark cherry in colour. He squatted

down and put it to his lips, his fingers, roughened by staff
and knife, suddenly appearing light and delicate as they
caressed it. Then he started to play.

7

When Tanith saw the place that her two captors called home, she nearly turned tail and fled. Only the knowledge that she couldn't outrun them made her stay. No, she and Wulfie would want all their cunning to get away. Right now, she needed to pretend to be satisfied with what was on offer – and that was two ramshackle garages and a scrapyard with a broken-down caravan parked to one side. The yard was full of rusting, twisted metal, none of which looked useful for anything but melting down.

"What's all this for?" asked Tanith, politely.

The men laughed. "Cover," said the one who had tried to strangle her. "Cover for our other operations."

"What are they?"

"Never you mind, kid," said the other man. "The less you know the better. But hunting is one of them – and that's big."

"So what do you hunt?" asked Tanith, trying not to let her voice shake.

The man laughed again. "Anything that's worth hunting. Legal or illegal. Rats – obviously. Then there's foxes, badgers, squirrels, cats, birds, deer…"

"Deer?" said Tanith. "Here? In the middle of the city?"

"Course not, stupid. It isn't only us that's hunting. We do city stuff – other blokes do the country. Look."

With that, he unlocked and raised the screeching metal door on one of the garages.

"Get in there – quick! You'll soon see."

Inside the garage, to Tanith's amazement, the space was kitted out like an office – a shabby one, it was true, but an office, nonetheless. There was even a grubby carpet on the floor.

"We sell to the Cratz," said the man. "Big business. That's our speciality stuff, of course. The scrawny stuff, the offal – that goes to the Citz – supposing they can come up with the dosh. So don't be expecting any of our best cuts of meat. A kid like you – you can have what even the Citz don't want."

Tanith gulped. Until that moment she hadn't

appreciated all that she had lost when her grandmother died. So now she wasn't even seen as a Citz – not even one of the desperately poor and oppressed victims of the Cratz's selfish hold on their world. Now she was only fit to eat the Citz's rejects. The thought made her retch.

"Where do I sleep?" she asked quickly. For reply, the man kicked open a door at the back of the office. Behind it was a tiny, galley-like kitchenette. At the far end was a small, beaten-up sofa.

"There," the man said, pointing. "And a lot better than most stray kids get, I can tell you. No heating here at night, of course, but just think – you could be in a cave like those vermin t'other side of the river."

"What vermin? What cave?"

"Kids. Like you. Strays and outcasts. Some of them squat in the old caves and bomb shelters over the other side of the river. Freezing cold, damp and miserable, I'd say. If you're thinking better of loaning your dog to us, just think about where you could end up."

Tanith shuddered. Nevertheless, a freezing cold cave on the other side of the river had its attractions. Anywhere so long as it was away from these appalling men with their poisonous breath.

"What's in the garage next door?" she asked, determined to keep up her brave face.

"Never you mind. You keep out of there, you hear me? Very, very cold it is in there. Perfect for our best cuts. And it's got a nice, deep pit for specialities. Old inspection pit.

Very deep. Very chilly. Just right for people who get too nosy or can't keep their mouths shut, you get me?" The man had his face up close to Tanith's now, his yellow and black teeth bared, his breath becoming hers.

She nodded vigorously, trying not to inhale. So next door was a big freezer. Her mind boggled at the size of this operation. She wouldn't have believed there were enough edible animals roaming the streets to fill that garage once, let alone repeatedly. But then maybe all this hunting talk was a bluff. Other operations. That's what he'd said. That must be what the second garage was really for. Whatever. She didn't intend staying long enough to find out. But the men mustn't know that.

"If I'm staying," she said, "you'd better tell me your names."

The man who had tried to capture Wulfie looked shifty. "No need for names," he said. "Just call me The Boss. Him – you can call him Sarge. He was in the army once – didn't get to be sergeant, of course." He laughed humourlessly and Sarge grunted. "But it'll help you to know *your* place. Bottom of the ranks, right? The lowest of the low."

Wulfie, who had been quiet, glued to Tanith's side, growled as he felt her stiffen angrily.

"I thought you wanted me to teach my dog to obey you," Tanith said, her eyes flashing.

"Ooh – hoity-toity," said The Boss, clearly enjoying her fury. "See here, Sarge. P'raps she'd like us to call her Corporal? Corporal Runt – how about that then?"

Tanith held Wulfie's collar. There was a very audible rumbling, deep in his throat. "Call me that again and I'll set him on you," she said. Wulfie had never been set on anything bigger than a fox in his life – but The Boss didn't need to know that.

The Boss held up his hands in mock surrender. "Hey – now, now, kiddo – no need to get shirty," he said. "Can't we take a little joke?"

Tanith decided that a dignified silence was her best response. Wulfie was tugging to get out of this hole. She followed him back under the metal door and into the yard. Immediately, he started sniffing and whining at the door of the other garage.

The Boss, who had followed them, laughed. "He's not stupid then. Knows what we've got stored away in there, I shouldn't wonder." Then he turned on Tanith. "But don't you ever let him in. Never, got it? And you neither. If I catch either of you in that store, then I'll shut you in and you'll be dead meat like the rest of it. Slow way to go, freezing. Don't tempt me, right? Got that?"

Tanith nodded. Suddenly, her eyes were smarting. She was remembering another freezing cold place with someone dead in it. Less than a week ago, that someone had been alive and she and Wulfie had been safe, fed and warm. Could it really be only a few days? It felt like a different life. Tanith snorted angrily, forcing back snot and tears. She had to be strong. This was no time for regret. She and Wulfie had to get out of this place and move on.

Only she knew Grandma's secret. She had been sent on a mission, one that only she could carry out. However dangerous it was, she and Wulfie had to escape from this hellhole as soon as they possibly could.

8

Crow didn't go back to his squat that day. He was too restless to sleep and too anxious to eat. At some point he must go and fish or Asta would be justifiably angry. It was unfair to spend so much time and energy on this one scrap of a girl when there were so many other kids relying on him.

He spent the daylight hours searching, trying to be discreet and failing. He was a known creature of the night. With his sharp dark looks and distinctive build he was an easy figure to spot and one that, because unfamiliar in the light, was conspicuous. He tried holing up with some of his young friends and sending them out on the prowl but the waiting was torture. While he hid away, anything could be happening to the girl and the dog. He was tired out and his mind wandered along dark paths. There were always rumours about what happened to the street kids that went missing, some more horrific than others. It was impossible for him not to dwell on them. In any case, it was soon obvious that word of his search was out. So he might as well do the job himself.

It was late afternoon, just when Crow had decided he must see what he could catch in the murky, contaminated canal, that he heard a whistle and his name called. He stopped and turned cautiously, instantly alert, his hand ready on the blade in his belt. It was an obvious trick – your name was called, you hesitated and the next minute someone jumped you, even in broad daylight. But he thought he recognized the voice; he thought this call was genuine.

It was a boy on a butcher's bike, the basket piled high with parcels. He didn't stop but raised his eyebrow and tilted his chin. *This way*, he was suggesting. Casually, as if he were merely continuing his walk, Crow followed.

The boy turned the bike into a ginnel. When Crow surreptitiously turned too, he found him waiting, his legs astride the bike, ready to go at a moment's notice.

This wasn't one of Crow's protégés. This lad was older than him. In the past, they had fought over busking pitches and had gained each other's respect. Jed had landed a job with a butcher since; he was one of the very few lucky ones who came to the city and finally found work.

"Hear you're looking for someone," said Jed. He was wary, his eyes flickering this way and that. "Girl like a duck and a big dog? That it?"

Privately, Crow thought the duck tag harsh but he wasn't going to argue. He nodded.

"What's your price?" he asked.

Jed shook his head. "No price."

Crow couldn't hide his surprise.

Jed's face was dark. "No price because you've got to rescue her. The blokes that have got her – they're evil. And the last thing they need is a big dog to help them."

Crow swallowed. So. The worst had happened, just as he had suspected it would. Jed worked for a butcher. Not all butchers were straight. Even those who were would know what the warped guys were up to.

"You're sure about this?"

Jed nodded. His voice was very low, barely more than a whisper.

"Meet me at midnight – St. Mary's churchyard. We'll go from there. I know where their outfit is. Bring Asta – we'll need someone to keep watch."

Crow nodded again. "You're certain you want to do this?" he asked, trying to read the look in Jed's eyes, trying to make sure this wasn't a trap. To his astonishment, Jed's eyes were moist.

"I've never been more sure about anything in my life," he said, dashing his hand angrily across his nostrils. "I'm a butcher, Crow. I know what goes on. I've seen it. It isn't rumour any more. It's the truth."

"Kid-catchers?" Crow whispered, his voice as light and chilled as a thread of frost.

"Murderers," said Jed.

Darkness had settled when Crow got back to the caves. Asta was squatting by the fire, tending a huge pot that had begun life as an oilcan. Had she forgiven him yet? Would she come with him and Jed that night? He hoped the squelching plastic bag that dangled heavily from his hand and that he'd had to defend fiercely as he crossed the city, would soften her. The kids who were already gathered, big-eyed and hopeful round the fire, spotted it and cheered.

"Asta, Asta! Crow's got us something!" one cried. The others were already crowding round him, emitting squeals of excitement. Asta stood up and turned. Hands on hips, she rocked back, raising an eyebrow sceptically.

"So!" she drawled. "The conquering hero returns. No kid and no dog and no money but perhaps a bag of rotting veg to go with the two onions I'm cooking?"

Crow smiled, hoping she was teasing, his teeth a surprising flash of white in the darkness. "I met Jed," he said. "The butcher's lad. It's liver and lights for us tonight, kids! Here, Asta, catch!"

He swung the bag, making as if to throw it to her, but

Asta cast him a look that might as well have been spit. "Cook it yourself," she snarled and stalked away, seeking the sanctuary of her own cave further along the riverbank.

Crow winced. He'd never seen her so upset with him. But the kids were clamouring round, desperate for a share of Jed's goodies and if he didn't act quickly, the onions would be burned. He grabbed the long, worn, paddle-like stick that Asta had been using, stirred the contents of the pot, and then tipped the slithering mass of offal into it. It hissed wickedly but immediately the night air was filled with the enticing smell of frying meat and onions. The kids drew closer, smacking their lips. Crow could almost feel their delight, snuggling round him, live and warm. It made his throat ache – it was pathetic, heartbreaking to see these waifs so thrilled by a pile of butcher's waste. But that was better than becoming it themselves.

Tonight, he would get the girl and the dog back – failing wasn't an option. The longer he stayed in this city, the more evil it became. He didn't know how much longer he could protect the motley band of kids that came his way if what Jed said was really true. He'd been hearing these rumours for months; this was the first time there'd been confirmation that they were true. But he had to try. It was that or… He shook his head, angrily. No. That was not the way out of this. He had been there and it was no better – in its way, it was worse. But he was running out of choices. How much longer could he hold out? How fair was it to keep his secret from all these little kids? Shouldn't he let them make up their minds themselves? Well, tonight he would find out how big the threat really was. First, however, he needed to win back Asta.

9

I am used to noises at night. My straw mattress rustles and so does that of my parents. My little truckle bed which pulls out from under the big bed, is strung beneath with rope that creaks. My father snores, the dog snuffles and snorts and, deep in the wattle and daub of the walls, mice tease our Puss as she paces.

Or they did until today when we found her, gory and torn, her throat ripped and her eyes glassy. The dog – maybe he was defending her, they had a certain respect for each other – is nursing a torn ear and a deep bite in his foreleg.

It is hard to settle to sleep. I add my own snuffles and sobs to the sounds of the night. Puss was a friend, softness and warmth in my harsh, cold life. My parents are abed before my eyes finally close and then it is to dreams barely different from waking, full of mangled fur and blood, beady little eyes and sharp, yellow teeth.

A crash, a broken pot wakes me. I start up with a yell and all around me in the dark I can hear skittering and yittering, snooping and whooping. My father strikes a light and there they all are, fat and triumphant, partying on our tabletop, swarming across the floor, snaffling our meagre supply of food and fouling our crockery with pee.

Father rises roaring, grabs a broom and a shovel. Mother follows, dragging me from my bed. The dog watches, licking his wounds, defeated.

Tanith woke, revolted and queasy. Her stomach was aching with hunger. The Boss said there would be food in the morning after she had started teaching Wulfie to work for them. She clutched her belly and sat up slowly, not sure if a sudden movement might make her retch, breathing carefully, and reaching with her free hand for the reassurance of Wulfie's rough fur. His warm tongue met her fingers and she pulled away with a gasp, plunged once again into her nightmare. His puzzled whine brought her back and, ignoring her griping pains, she swung herself off the low couch so that she could snuggle her whole body hard into his grizzled coat.

But Wulfie was still whining, his body tense, hunched, ready to spring, his ears pricked.

"What is it, Wulfie?" Tanith whispered, stroking him soothingly. "Heard something? Probably only a rat." Maybe that was what had triggered her awful dream.

And then she heard something too. Not a definable noise. Not a running rat or a stealthy footstep. Maybe something being dropped, maybe someone banging against something in the yard. Instantly, Tanith was alert, all shreds of sleepiness gone, straining to understand what her ears were telling her.

Nothing. Right now, she could hear absolutely nothing. Wulfie was still poised, waiting, however. Whatever was out there hadn't gone.

It could, of course, be a passing fox or something falling over in the breeze. But Tanith didn't think Wulfie would be so tense if that was all it was. Some sort of intruder then – but who? Tanith didn't like to think. The Boss's talk of big business, cover and other operations was terrifying. He could have scores of enemies. She dismissed the idea of a police raid instantly. The police – those who weren't corrupt – had, she thought, got quite enough to do keeping order on the streets. That they should have sussed out The Boss's seedy operations on just the night she needed them to seemed quite beyond the bounds of probability. No, it was far more likely that one of The Boss's competitors was on the prowl – or maybe someone who had a grudge against him. In which case, what should she do – keep quiet and hide or throw herself upon their mercy? Mercy seemed unlikely – especially for Wulfie. Tanith had learned horribly quickly how valuable he had become. The sensible thing to do was to stay quiet, tucked away in the kitchen, and hope that the intruders wouldn't notice the doorway. She wrapped her hands round Wulfie's muzzle and sat tight, whispering to him to be quiet and hoping she could hold him if he chose to disobey.

A few minutes of dead silence followed. Sarge had been left on guard in the broken-down caravan; she didn't suppose there was a loo in there – maybe he'd gone out to the yard. Why hadn't she thought of that before?

Tanith had just decided to crawl back onto the couch and try to sleep once more, when she felt Wulfie's body vibrate. A barely audible grumble started in his chest. At times like these, she cursed her awkward legs and the night-time stiffness of her joints. She felt as if the intruder would hear her very bones clunking. She pushed the door open a crack and instantly heard what was bothering Wulfie. Someone was trying to break in to the garage.

Tanith froze, her hands clamped round Wulfie's jaw. Should she shout for help from Sarge, start hammering on the tiny window of the kitchenette, let Wulfie loose to bark his head off? But who wanted to be rescued by Sarge? Could this intruder be any worse? Wouldn't she be better to take her chance, explain what was going on and hope for the best?

She had seconds to decide. At any moment, the lock could give. The kitchenette was bare of anything that could usefully make a weapon and the garage was in pitch-darkness. Tanith pushed open the connecting door, flicked on the kitchen light and scanned the office frantically. Grabbing the only moveable item – an old-fashioned tin litter bin – she advanced towards the garage door, just as the lock finally gave and someone pushed against it.

Tanith waited, her heart hammering, one hand on Wulfie's collar, the other awkwardly clutching the bin. It had a promisingly sharp rim; that could do some damage. The up-and-over door opened a few centimetres at the bottom and then stopped. From outside, she could hear whispering. She picked out the word "light" and that was all. So they'd noticed the kitchen light go on. Whoever it was now knew they weren't dealing with an empty garage. She had given herself away. Now what?

More urgent whispering. Tanith's eyes were getting accustomed to the dim light coming from the kitchen. She crouched low, keeping back, waiting.

Outside she could see two sets of beaten up DMs. The legs that rose from them wore jeans. You couldn't tell much from that except that one pair of DMs was smaller than the other.

Tanith had been expecting heavies – something similar to The Boss and Sarge. She peered under the door again, straining to hear what was being said and struggling to keep hold of Wulfie.

At that moment, something very unexpected happened. A slender hand slid under the door and deposited – a fish!

There was no holding Wulfie then. Tanith had only one hand on his collar and he was as hungry as she was.

"No, Wulfie," she yelled, the fear of poison scattering all caution, but he lunged forward regardless and the fish was in his mouth before she had even dropped the bin with a giveaway clang.

In those seconds, someone pushed the screaming garage door open fully and someone else pounced and hauled her out.

"Friends," that person hissed. "Now run!"

Faced with no option and the sounds of Sarge waking and banging his way out of the caravan, Tanith did exactly that. Wulfie, the fish devoured in one gulp, bounded past her. The yard gates were ajar, their chain cut. Tanith dashed through the gap.

"Here!" called another voice and there was a thickset boy on a bicycle. "Quick!" he said. "Get up!"

Somehow Tanith managed to scramble onto the saddle. Occasionally, she had done this with kids in the village. They rode standing, while she desperately hung on, clinging to their backs with her arms and trying to find somewhere, anywhere to rest her feet. The ride had never lasted long before ending in a tumble.

"I don't think I can do this," she said to the back of the boy.

"Just hold tight," he said. "It's not far."

Tanith had forgotten the garages were at the top of a hill. The next moment, the bike was careering down it, the boy standing on the pedals, freewheeling precariously, while she clung on, her cheek pressed so hard against his back that she could feel every thread in his jacket. She dug the sides of her legs into the icy, bruising metal of the frame, completely failing to find a foothold. She had to stay on that bike. She daren't lift her head to look and could only hope that Wulfie was with them, bounding ahead or behind. Up the hill, she could hear an engine starting. Sarge would be after them in moments. Whoever the boy was and whoever his accomplices were, staying with them was her only hope of survival. Sarge, she knew, wouldn't think twice about finishing her off, now that she'd broken the deal.

10

The bike ride ended where the road bridged the river at the bottom of the hill. The boy skidded to a halt with a squeal of brakes and Tanith crashed painfully into his back, scraping her legs on the pedals.

"Get off," said the boy, as if she had any choice. "Get down that bank."

Beside the bridge, there was a short, steep drop to the river, slippery with frost, the sort of unofficial path that kids beat when they needed a short cut. Tanith didn't argue but, wary of her awkward gait, crouched down and slid the few metres on her bottom. Wulfie tobogganed after her, narrowly avoiding rolling her into the water.

Tanith looked up but the boy on the bike was gone. For a moment or two, she was alone, stunned and bewildered, unable to think of anything apart from the crazy beating of her heart, which was so violent it terrified her. Then another boy slid down the slope and, right behind him, a girl. Tanith recognized their DMs and… She blinked and had to look again. Surely the boy was the very one who had tried to steal Wulfie in the woods?

"This way," panted the girl and they shot under the bridge, dragging Tanith behind them, just as Sarge's van drove over it. They hugged the wall, barely breathing during the seconds when they thought he might stop. He drove on, stupidly, Tanith thought. Hadn't he seen them dive off the road?

The boy let out a gasp. "Good. He thinks she's still on the bike with Jed."

"Dimwit," said the girl.

"Yeah. Luckily," said the boy. "But we can't hang around."

The girl gave Tanith a shove and they were moving again, along the rusty cinder track that clung to the river. Grim, dilapidated buildings rose on either side. Tanith had a sinking feeling that she was following these kids out of the frying pan into the fire but she could see no other option. When the girl reached a small, decaying rowing boat which seemed to sit in the thick, oily water like a dead fly on cold custard, she hesitated. The one thing she'd never persuaded her recalcitrant body to do was swim and the idea of all four of them crammed into the tiny vessel seemed like suicide.

The girl leaped in confidently, waited for the rocking to stop, and held out her hand. Tanith looked at her helplessly. With her short legs and stiffness, she could do nothing but fall into the boat. The boy didn't hesitate. He hoicked her up under her arms and lowered her over the riverbank. Tanith didn't dare protest.

"Help me, Asta!" he said and the girl, clearly unimpressed, guided Tanith's legs and helped her thump down into the tub. It rocked alarmingly and had barely settled before, with a whimper and a leap, Wulfie nearly capsized it.

"God!" said the girl. "Make him sit down."

"Sit, Wulfie, sit," Tanith gasped and, to her immense relief, he subsided on the floor between the seat where she had collapsed and the one on which the hostile girl was now perched, an oar in each hand.

The boy had unfastened the rope and was pushing them off.

"See you later," he said. "Take care."

"Of myself or of her?" the girl muttered, leaning forward aggressively to let the oars dip into the water. As she pulled back, making the boat shoot away smoothly, she glared at Tanith.

"I hope you're worth all this trouble," she said.

Tanith didn't reply. Her heart was still hammering from the terror of the last ten minutes. Even if she'd been able to find her voice, she wouldn't have known what to say in the face of the girl's antagonism. Instead, Tanith hung on hard to Wulfie's collar, digging her fingers into his fur for comfort and wondering why on earth she'd been rescued by a girl who seemed to hate her and the strange, sharp-boned boy she'd met in the woods.

Crow, eagle-eyed for trouble, slid fleet-footed through the dangerous dark places that ran down to the waterline at the edge of the city centre. These were the haunts of the unlucky ones, street kids who got caught up in a lethal underworld of drug rings and other malevolent gangs, lorded over by adults who had once been street kids themselves and others who had fallen foul of their deeply divided world – the privileged, protected Cratz and the powerless, poverty-stricken Citz, eking out a precarious existence in the broken city.

Crow swerved to avoid a stick-thin arm, thrust out from a bundle of rags huddled in a damp corner. His heart clenched with a mixture of pity and terror. The terror kept him moving. There were places and times for him to offer what compassion he could. Here and now wasn't one of them. Anything pitiful could be a trap for the unwary and anyway, tonight he had a different mission. Strapped across his back, he had his firestaffs. Despite the fact that his body ached, his eyes stung and his head was muzzy from lack of sleep, tonight he would busk for the throngs of reckless young Cratz spilling out from the nightclubs. He needed the money and, more importantly, he wanted the word out that he was back, that he had failed in his search and that the girl with the dog had gone, hell and its demons alone knew where. He didn't suppose he could stave off pursuit for long but he needed to buy whatever time he could. He just hoped Asta could get the pair safely to the caves under cover of the night. It had been her idea to use the boat and he was still unsure whether he should have trusted her. The idea had sprung up in the middle of a terrible row.

It had started after he had fed the children the offal that Jed had provided and he had attempted to take Asta a plateful as a peace offering. He had hovered at the entrance to her cave, hoping the smell would entice her out. It hadn't and, tentatively, he had pushed aside the old curtain she had retrieved from a dump and hung up on rusting nails dug into the soft sandstone. He could barely see in the gloom for she hadn't bothered to waste a light to cheer her misery.

"Asta?" he said. "Are you there?"

There was a rustle and something that sounded suspiciously like a sob.

"Yes," said Asta. "What do you want?"

"I've brought you some food."

Asta, however moody, was never stupid. She wouldn't starve herself for the sake of a sulk.

"I'm over here."

"Where? I can't really see."

"Well, I can. Hold the plate out, idiot."

Crow was backlit by the night sky beyond the cave door. He held out the plate, ruefully contemplating how very far short he was of his usual alertness. In another situation, someone could have taken advantage of his visibility to jump him.

His eyes were acclimatizing to the gloom now and he could see Asta sitting cross-legged on her makeshift bedding roll. Shoulders hunched, chin down, she shovelled in the food silently.

"I'm sorry, Asta," he said. "I know you think I'm being stupid. Do you mind if I sit down?"

Crow was always respectful of Asta's space. He knew how much he valued his own. He also knew that it was one of the reasons Asta stuck by him, even at times like this when he felt as if she hated his guts. Their deal was simple – she kept a daytime watch on his waifs and strays and in return he provided for her and offered a certain amount of protection. That was all. He was struggling to see why she was taking his concern for the girl and her dog quite so hard. She was always grumpy when there was a new mouth to feed but she was too good-hearted to let it last. He had expected pity for the girl to win through by now.

Asta shuffled along her bedding roll and Crow squatted on the end. Her face, resolutely fixed on her food and shrouded by stray curls, was uninviting but Crow had to speak. He took a deep breath.

"Asta, I need your help."

She snorted. "When don't you?"

He sighed. "I know, I know. But this is different. I need your help tonight. Jed knows where the girl and the dog are."

That got her head up.

"Where?"

"Some lock-up garages, the other side of the river."

"This end of the city?"

"No, the other."

"What d'you want me for?"

"Lookout. That's what Jed thought." Crow knew as he said it, it was a mistake.

"Lookout? Lookout? Typical no-brained boy! Take one of your kids if you want a lookout! Why bother me?"

"I don't know. Jed just thought—"

"Jed didn't think at all. What else has he thought? Has he thought how you're going to get that kid and her monster dog through the city centre without being spotted? Has he thought how you're going to get into a lock-up garage? Has he thought how many heavies might be guarding the place?"

Crow's brain flailed helplessly. No, they hadn't thought through any of those things. They hadn't planned beyond meeting at St. Mary's. All he himself had thought about was how he might get Asta on side and so far he was failing miserably.

"Give me strength," Asta spat. "Do either of you know how to pick a lock?"

"Jed might."

"Jed might. Great. So I'm to keep watch while Jed 'might' be able to pick a lock but actually gets us all caught red-handed by some random bunch of thugs! Then what? Supposing by some miracle we get away with this kid that walks at a snail's pace and this dog that's about as inconspicuous as a stinking Citz beggar at a Cratz wedding? Do I keep watch while the heavies club you all to death? Is that it?"

Crow sprang to his feet. "All right, all right," he said, his voice taut with irritation. He was tired, overwrought and cross with himself for being so naïve about the difficulties. "You don't want to help. Jed and I will manage. I'll get one of the kids to be lookout. You just stay here and – and – do your mending or something!"

For reply, Asta spat on the ground.

"How dare you?" she cried. "How dare you sneer at me like that? You come here, wanting me to help you with your crack-brained scheme and when I point out a few flaws, you treat me like an idiot! Just tell me, if I wasn't here, how would you cope? What would you do then? Be 'mum' all day and 'dad' all night? I don't think so. Hasn't it occurred to you for one moment that if you want to inflict this disabled kid on us, you might at least discuss it with me?"

Crow stepped back, appalled by Asta's fury but seething himself. He really didn't need this now. He was tired out, anxious and desperate for Asta to cooperate. He knew how he could solve this but was too exhausted and unsettled to try.

"You need me tonight," Asta continued. "And not to keep watch. I can pick locks. And I can row."

"Row?" Crow was baffled. His brain wasn't making connections.

"Yes, idiot, row! In and out, splish, splash, what you do on a river, okay? With me now? That's the only way to get the pair of them past the city."

"What about a boat?"

"I know where I can get one."

They stood there, a metre apart, with nothing between them except their pain. It hurt to be at such odds with each other. Then Asta half-reached out her hand towards Crow but he turned away, deliberately avoiding her eyes. *No, Asta,* he thought irritably, nursing his anger. *So you feel bad now. Live with it. I'm not going to help.*

"Right then," he said walking away. "It sounds like a plan. I'll tell Jed."

11

I am sitting by the river, rod in hand, waiting. I am good at waiting, good at fishing. It is one of the few things my ungainly body can do well, one of the few ways I can get a word of praise tossed my way by my father. But the fish are slow to bite today; they seem determined to lie low, skulking and sulking, refusing the temptation of my juicy worm-bait. Maybe they sense what is coming before I do and, sensibly, take cover.

I am glad to get out of the town today where everyone has been agog and aquiver. I don't like crowds, unstable and short as I am, and a huge mob has gathered in the marketplace. Someone has come, a strange character in outlandish robes, claiming to be able to rid us of our trouble – for a fee, of course. I don't like him – don't trust him. But the mayor offered him fifty thousand gold coins! Fifty thousand! And no one argued. Not one.

But now I feel the people coming – or I think it is them, anyway. Either that or an army on the move. I can feel the vibration of the earth in the bank where I sit. I crane my neck but before I see anything I hear something, a thin, reedy sound, almost too high for me to register.

And then, ahead of the sound, something else is advancing upon me – something worse than the stuff of my nightmares. It is a brown, heaving tide, surging towards me. Not a huge wave or a massive bore, just a low, creeping, murky tide, racing towards the riverbank with a relentlessness which appals me. I am right in its path. There will be no stopping it knocking me off my unsteady legs and driving me over the bank into the restless river where I will inevitably drown, choked by the water I have never learned to master and suffocated by that mass of brown.

Suddenly, it is upon me, breaking in loathsome ripples of filthy fur, crazed, gleaming eyes and sharp, scrabbling claws. I fall, tripping on lashing tails and am at once over the bank, clutching at tufts of grass, roots, anything that will stop me falling into the churning water along with the frantic creatures who swarm over me, under me, round me, thankfully ignoring me in their race to hit the river.

I hang there, arms at breaking point, stiff legs scrabbling for a foothold, while the water boils with bobbing bodies, only a whisker's breadth from my toes.

The sudden bump of the boat against the bank jolted Tanith awake. For a moment, she didn't know where she was and then the sight of the girl, glaring at her beneath her raggle-taggle curls, brought back everything with such a rush that she felt sick.

"Come on," said the girl, curtly. "This way."

"I'm sorry," said Tanith, struggling to her feet in the rocking boat, using Wulfie's broad back for support. "A minute – I feel ill."

The girl tossed her head impatiently but she busied herself with making the boat fast while Tanith took some deep breaths. Then the girl held out a hand and helped her ashore. It was a huge relief to Tanith that here the path was almost on a level with the boat. She already felt such an idiot compared with her strong, capable, striking rescuer that she wasn't sure she could bear the humiliation of being hauled ignominiously up the bank. *Stupid*, she told herself. *You've just escaped from the most evil men you've ever met and you're worried that you look like a loser?*

"I'm Tanith," she said when she was safely on land. "And this is Wulfie."

"Asta," said the girl.

"And the boy?"

Asta didn't question which one. "Crow."

"I've met him before," Tanith ventured.

"I know."

Tanith was desperate to ask why they'd rescued her, how they knew where she was, what they wanted with her, but Asta was scrambling up a steep, sandy path. Her back looked so forbidding that Tanith kept quiet and focused on getting her frozen, aching joints to behave. She didn't know how long she'd slept in the boat but hours curled up in the unheated garage followed by that damp journey had taken their toll. She had to bite her lips to stop herself moaning with pain as she struggled after Asta.

Mercifully, the path was short and they quickly arrived at a wide dusty ledge, at the centre of which the embers of a fire glowed beneath a makeshift tripod bearing an old oilcan. The aroma of cooked meat and onions still hung in the heavy, freezing air, making Tanith's mouth water and Wulfie drool.

"Wait here," said Asta and she suddenly seemed to vanish into the cliff wall which rose at the far side of the ledge. The next moment she was back and Tanith's tired brain had made a connection. Vermin that lived in caves. That was what The Boss had said. So the vermin had rescued her. But why would such desperate kids, who must have to scratch and scrimp to survive, bother? Not out of simple kindness, surely?

Asta was scraping the bottom of the oilcan with a big

stick. She then spread the scrapings onto something leathery that she held in her hand.

"Oatcake and offal," she said, holding it out to Tanith. "It's all we've got."

Tanith didn't care. "Thank you," she said. "You're very kind."

Asta tossed back her hair. "No, I'm not," she said. "Well, not particularly. That's Crow's thing – kindness. He'd want me to give you something to eat."

"Won't he be back soon?" asked Tanith. She had hoped he might have got there ahead of them. Being alone with Asta made her nervous. At least the boy Crow had tried to warn her of the dangers of the city.

"Crow? No – he works at night. Didn't last night, of course – he was looking for you – so he needs to work tonight. Or we'll have nothing to eat."

"Oh," said Tanith, feeling guilty. Maybe that was the reason for Asta's hostility. Hunger was never good for the temper.

"Maybe it's different where you come from?" said Asta. "Enough food if you've got the money?"

Tanith shook her head. "I'm not Cratz, if that's what you mean. I lived in the hills. The land is pretty barren but there are sheep and you can grow some vegetables still. Anyway, why would a Cratz come here?"

Asta shrugged. "Occasionally they do. Their parents die of the sickness – I know they have some drugs but they don't often work. They've no relatives and don't want to be put in a home. Sometimes they just feel stifled in the enclaves. Mad, if you ask me. I'd rather feel stifled than hungry all the time – but then they don't know what that feels like till they come here."

"Well, I certainly do," said Tanith.

"You're in luck then," said Asta. "Jed gave us liver and lights. That's what you've got there."

"It's very good," said Tanith gratefully, shovelling down the last of the oatcake. She longed to ask at least some of the questions that surged in her head but was all too aware that she was keeping her rescuer waiting.

"Right, this way," said Asta and led her across the ledge and inside one of the arches dug out of the rock face. She had snatched a glowing brand from the dying fire but it didn't shed much light. Tanith could dimly see a metre or so ahead but that was all. She had no idea of the dimensions of the tunnel they had entered but was instantly chilled through by the penetrating damp. This would not be a comfortable night. Wulfie hugged her legs, clearly as unnerved as she was.

After a short distance, Asta turned a corner. "Here'll do for tonight," she said. "I couldn't find much for a blanket but your dog should keep you warm. Go on – lie down. I'll see you in the morning."

By the dim light of the brand, Tanith could see a clear patch on the dirt floor, close to the wall and covered with cardboard. Next to it lay a huddled, sleeping child. Something was bunched up for a pillow and there was an old jacket too which Tanith assumed would be her only covering. She nearly screamed when a voice suddenly spoke from the darkness ahead.

"Is it another new kid, Asta?"

"Timbo, aren't you asleep?" said Asta.

"It's hard," said the voice, plaintively. "It's so dark and it scares me."

"Do you like dogs?" asked Tanith, her heart going out to this kid she couldn't even see. "Cos if you do, come and share mine. I'd be scared of the dark too without him."

"Can I, Asta?" said the voice. "Is that okay?"

"Of course," said Asta, her tone the warmest Tanith had heard it. "There's plenty of space here for both of you."

Then, out of the darkness, a small boy stumbled, dragging a large piece of cardboard and a ratty-looking blanket.

"Lie down, Wulfie," said Tanith and with a great sigh, he did. Then she and the boy snuggled up either side of him and Asta bid them goodnight.

Despite having Wulfie to hang on to, Tanith's eyes clung to the glimmering brand until the very last moment, when Asta turned the corner. Then the darkness was complete.

"What's your name?" said the little boy, suddenly.

"Tanith."

"That's nice. Thank you for letting me share your big dog, Tanith."

"That's okay, Timbo."

Tanith had her arm wrapped firmly round Wulfie, her

hand gripping his fur, her eyes tight shut so that she couldn't see how dark it was.

"Tanith," said Timbo, in a voice which wobbled. "Can I hold your hand?"

"Of course," said Tanith. "It's here – near Wulfie's collar."

Timbo's hand was warm and soft. Tanith could tell by its plumpness that he hadn't been in the city long. She grasped it with her own stubby, hardened fingers and hoped that was reassuring. Maybe it was, because a few moments later she felt Timbo relax and his breathing turned deep and steady. Suddenly, Tanith was utterly exhausted and, despite the frightening tomb-like feel of her bed, she fell into a deep and dreamless sleep, comforted herself by the warm little hand in hers.

12

Tanith woke to Wulfie's excited yelping and his big tongue washing her face. She had been so deeply asleep, smothered by the extreme darkness of the tunnel, that she felt as if she had slept for days. She groped her way out, realizing that they were a surprisingly short distance from the entrance. The biting chill of the outside air quickly cleared her head and she saw, from the streaky greyness of the wintry light, that it was still early morning; in fact, only a few hours had passed since her escape.

Outside the tunnel, rather to her resentment, Wulfie was

gambolling about, greeting Crow with the enthusiasm of a long-lost friend. He was completely shameless, she thought, won over with a few tainted fish. She was determined to be much more cautious. To her annoyance, she was stiff and unsteady and had to sit down, leaning awkwardly against the cliff face.

"Here, Wulfie," she called, her voice cold. Crow may have rescued her but she didn't know why and Asta's attitude hadn't exactly inspired confidence. Reluctantly, Wulfie slunk back to her side but whined at her wistfully, his big eyes puzzled.

Crow advanced hesitantly. To Tanith's surprise, he seemed nervous. She immediately noticed the pallor of his face and how dark the shadows were beneath his heavy eyes. He was seriously short of sleep and all because of her. Why?

For a moment, he looked directly into her eyes. The look was so sharp, so penetrating and so unexpected from someone who seemed so weary, that she was taken aback. She felt strangely unbalanced, as if the floor had tipped slightly. In that second, she could see how well his name suited him. It wasn't just his physique; there was something uncannily powerful, almost predatory in his gaze. But the look passed, his eyes dropped and suddenly he was just a very tired and grubby-looking teenager, kicking at the dirt.

"I'm Crow," he said. "We met in the woods."

"Yes," said Tanith. "You tried to steal my dog." He might

as well know that she didn't trust him.

"Will you tell me your name?"

"Tanith."

"Tanith? I haven't heard that before."

"So? It's no more unusual than Crow or Asta."

Crow shrugged. "Maybe we're unusual people. You certainly are."

Tanith bridled instantly. "What do you mean by that?" she demanded. "You've got a problem with my disability?"

Crow held his hands up in appeal. "Woah, slow down," he said. "I'm sorry – no offence intended. I didn't mean that at all."

"What then? What?"

She regretted the words even as she was saying them. She hated drawing attention to her limitations. Normally, she lived peaceably enough with her chronic pain but there were times when its intensity made it difficult to cope. This was one. She was tense and ill at ease and had slept for too long on a damp, hard floor. It all conspired to make her snappish.

Crow passed a hand across his brow. "I'm sorry. I'm exhausted. I'm doing this all wrong. Can we start again?"

"Okay," said Tanith, still suspicious. "Why don't you begin by telling me why you went to all that trouble to rescue me?"

"I'd rather explain later. Right now, you need to get away. You won't be safe here for long. Those thugs will be trying to trace you. We need to get moving – the longer we stay here, the more at risk you are – and so are all the other kids that hang out here."

Tanith's heart quailed. Vermin that live in the caves. The Boss and Sarge and whoever else they worked with would have no qualms about wiping out vermin, she was sure.

"So why did you bring me here if I just make things dangerous?" she asked crossly. It was awful to feel responsible for other people's safety. She was thinking of little Timbo, clinging to her hand in the night. It made her stomach churn to think that her very presence might be endangering him.

"Really – it's a long story," said Crow. "Can you just try and trust me? Can we just go? I know you must be hungry and tired but we can deal with that later."

"Why should I trust you? You tried to steal my dog! And your friend Asta. Even if you did rescue me, it's obvious that she didn't want to."

Crow sighed. "I know – it's difficult. But please believe me – you're still in terrible danger. There are other people after your dog – the news is all over the city – and they won't think twice about killing you to get him. We need to leave."

Tanith began to haul herself to her feet but her cramped limbs and stiff joints weren't helping.

"Give me a hand then, please," she said. "I don't really have much choice, do I?"

Crow grabbed her wrists and pulled. As he did so, their eyes met, Tanith's wary and cross, Crow's puzzled and searching.

"I wish I could make you trust me," he said, his voice frustrated.

"Telling me what's going on would be a start," said Tanith.

"Maybe," said Crow. "Maybe not. Well, let's get going then."

Crow led Tanith along the rocky ledge until it petered out and they had to scramble down along the edge of the river, clinging to whatever handholds they could find, the water lapping less than half a metre below them and the bank so narrow that Tanith felt green with terror. Crow traversed quickly with the nimbleness of a monkey and regular practice; Tanith, unsupple and bruised, struggled to keep up. Crow waited for her where the bank widened into a rudimentary path.

"All right?" he asked, offering a hand as she stumbled on the last bit. She could see that he was hesitant, unsure whether to offer help. Hardly surprising, she thought, given the way she had bitten his head off for saying she was unusual. Proudly, she steadied herself against Wulfie who had taken the difficult sections in a few bounds, but her eyes smarted with tears.

They trudged along in silence, Crow beating back brambles with his firestaff.

"That's the way I came in, isn't it?" she ventured at last, "On the other side of the river? Didn't I go through those woods to get to the city?"

"What?" Crow stumbled slightly and turned, frowning

and rubbing his eyes. He had almost been asleep on his feet.

"I said, isn't that the way I came into the city? On the other side?"

"Yes, yes – of course. The track runs near the top of the slope. I'm taking you to my squat. No one knows where it is – not even Asta – so we should be okay there for a while. We can catch up on some sleep at least. But there's nowhere to cross till further up."

"Won't you tell me why you're doing this?" said Tanith. "I really don't get it. Is it Wulfie you want? I could understand that."

Crow stopped and turned. "Tanith, it's complicated," he said, "and I'm so tired I can hardly think straight. I promise I'll tell you later and I promise I'm not going to hurt you or your dog. Please can you be patient for a bit longer? It's not far now."

Tanith shrugged. "Okay then," she said. "Let's go." When he talked like that, he was so winsome – but even that felt threatening. He seemed too good to be true – so reasonable, so caring, so concerned about her and about the other kids. And anyway, there was her other image of him, burning staff in hand, giving her that unnerving stare, snarling at her to stay where she was and leaving her weak-kneed and woozy with shock. In stories, the most sinister villains were always the most charming.

They rounded a bend in the river and there, stretching in a gentle arc across it, was a rushing weir. Crow handed Tanith his firestaff and unslung his second one.

"This is where we cross," he said. "Take it slowly and you should be fine. It's smooth and firm and the water's not too fast today."

Tanith stared at Crow, open-mouthed in horror.

"I…I can't," she said. "And if I fall in, I can't swim."

Crow cast a glance sideways, tight-lipped. She could see that he was irritated. "It's the only way," he said. "It's really easy, honestly. I do it every day."

"It might be for you," Tanith retorted, "but I *don't* do it every day. And my legs don't work like yours do. I don't do balancing acts."

"You're tough though – I've seen you. You scramble like a goat. And you're fit. Besides, there isn't any choice – unless I try to carry you and, to be honest, I'm not sure my balance is up to that."

Tanith gulped. For a moment, she thought of begging him to, however bad his balance was, but her pride wouldn't let her.

"It's okay," she said. "Just give me a minute, all right?"

Instead, Crow strode towards her. Before she could defend herself, he took her chin in his hand and looked straight into her eyes.

"You can do this, Tanith," he said, and she felt as if his eyes were scouring hers. "Trust me, you can."

Tanith let out a small scream and pulled away. "No!" she exclaimed. "Don't do that!"

Crow let his hand drop, stung. "I'm sorry," he said,

flushing. "I didn't mean to startle you. I was trying to help."
He turned away.

"Well, you didn't," said Tanith, still keeping her distance.
She shook her head fiercely. She had a horrible sensation
as if her brain had been raked. *Don't be silly*, she told
herself. *Don't let this weird guy spook you. Remember he
rescued you from The Boss and Sarge. Now come on. You've
got to cross that weir. Live with it!*

"Well?" she said. "Are we doing this then?"

Crow looked up. "Yeh, I guess so," he said. He seemed
embarrassed, uncomfortable. "Do you...do you want a
hand?"

Tanith took a step back. "Let's just get on with it,"
she said.

Crow went first, striding out as if the weir was no different
from the path. In moments, he was across.

"You see?" he called back. "It's easy – honestly."

Tanith took a deep breath and clambered onto the rocky
ledge which formed the step in the river, using Crow's staff
to steady herself. The weir was as solid as Crow had
promised but slimy with sickly-looking moss and she could
feel the push of the current even though, where she stood,
the water ran only a few centimetres high. Slowly,
awkwardly, eyes fixed firmly ahead, she took a step and
then another. *Don't look down*, she told herself. *Don't look
down.* Below her the water churned and frothed, dizzying
her even though she could only glimpse it from the corner

of her eye. Within a few paces, her palms and her upper lip were sweating. She was inching her way along, not daring to do more than shuffle, her face set grimly, both fists clenched around the staff. She didn't dare look at Crow. It was humiliating to struggle like this after watching his limber performance. She thought of Asta and how she would have bounded across in a few graceful strides. Not for the first time, despite her pride in what she could make her difficult body do, she hated it. Wulfie, she knew, was right behind her. She could hear his whimper above the roar of the weir. Poor Wulfie. He too would like to leap across and get his feet out of the freezing water but loyally, he wouldn't leave her behind. A traitor tear crept down Tanith's cheek and she brushed it aside angrily. Fatal.

The sudden movement, the sudden loss of focus and her balance was gone. Her foot slipped and she was down on one knee, scrabbling at the slimy rock to drag her leg back and get upright again, desperately trying not to let Crow's staff slip away. She felt Wulfie's breath hot on her neck. He had her collar in his teeth and was holding her firm as she struggled, her other knee slipping in the rushing water which was pulling and dragging and freezing her so that she was losing what little grip she had.

You have to do this, she told herself, through clamped teeth. *You cannot die here.* But she was slipping, slipping, there was nothing for her hands to grab, there was only Wulfie tugging at her for all he was worth and she was too cold and tired and hurting to carry on.

13

"Tanith, I've got you. Use my legs! Forget the staff!"

Tanith grabbed Crow's ankles and heaved. He was pulling her up, Wulfie had her firm – between them they got her safely back onto the ledge but the firestaff had slipped from beneath Tanith's frozen fingers and sank quickly, pounded by the relentless weir.

"I'll carry you," said Crow.

"No," said Tanith, trying to pluck up the courage to let go of his legs. "I'll crawl."

"Tanith, you're shaking all over."

"I'm just cold."

"Tanith – please!"

"You said you didn't think you could carry me. What's different now? I'll be safer crawling. Just give me a minute."

Crow folded his arms and waited. Tanith, desperately trying to control the trembling which had invaded her whole body, couldn't help thinking how ridiculous she must look, on her knees, clinging to Crow's legs, half-soaked, her dog still hanging on to her collar as if she was a naughty puppy. It was unbearably embarrassing. But she would not even consider being carried now. That would complete her humiliation. With a massive effort, she let go of Crow and put her hands in the icy water.

"I'm ready," she said.

This time Crow walked slowly ahead, never more than an arm's length in front of Tanith, while she crawled painfully along, chewing her lips to prevent herself moaning. Her shins and fingers quickly grew so cold that she couldn't feel them and she began to worry that they would soon be useless to her. When she finally reached the far side and saw that she must now master a steep scramble onto the bank, she nearly howled in despair, but Crow didn't wait for her to argue and hauled until he had landed her.

For a moment or two she lay still, feeling as helpless as a wounded whale, fighting back tears of relief and pain.

She turned her face so that Wulfie could lick it with his warm tongue while Crow squatted beside her.

"I'll be fine in a minute," she said.

"I'm sorry," said Crow. "I didn't realize how hard it would be for you."

"Stop apologizing," said Tanith. "Please. It's getting boring. And I've lost your firestaff."

"It doesn't matter. Well, not much."

"Don't lie. How are you going to get another one? Asta'll go mad – I've cost you enough already."

"Don't worry about her – I'll sort it. Come on – we've got to get you warm and dry."

Tanith struggled to her feet. She could barely feel them and had to hold Wulfie to steady herself. As she began to walk, she was horribly aware of how stooped and clumsy she must look.

It wasn't far to Crow's squat but it was tortuously slow. Crow's face seemed to wince with every step Tanith took, building murderous thoughts in her heart. In the end, she caught his arm and shook it.

"Will you stop looking like that?" she cried. "I'm used to this. It looks bad, I know, but it's just the way I am. I don't need your pity, okay? Why don't you run ahead and do something useful like lighting a fire? I can manage on my own with Wulfie. He'll find you. And don't" – she had seen his mouth opening – "begin to apologize again. Just live with it, all right? I do!"

To her relief, Crow smiled briefly and then ran off. Tanith's whole body relaxed, easing the pain. Her lip trembled and a short sob escaped her but that was balm to her battered body. Pain was bad enough, without having to keep up a brave face.

After that, it didn't seem long before Wulfie was leading her off the path and into the bushes to find the abandoned mill. Inside it, prepared to run the risk of someone spotting the smoke for once, Crow had made a small fire, and was heating something in a pan. There was a heap of old clothes on the floor.

"Find something dry to wear and then come and eat," said Crow. "I won't look, honestly."

Tanith scanned the bare room. Unless she went outside, she would have to rely on his promise. She rummaged through the pile, hunting for the smallest things she could find. Crow was tall so it wasn't easy but she managed to find some jeans that she could roll up, a soft warm shirt, a body warmer and a rough, woolly jumper to pull over the whole lot. She found some thick socks in a mound of odd ones and some sheepskin mittens. Crow *was* kind. He talked gently and made no further comment about the lost firestaff – but she couldn't forget the way he had looked at her. Those eyes – so intense, so penetrating – there was something almost inhuman about them. She shuddered at the memory.

Quickly, Tanith pulled off her wet clothes, very self-conscious, despite Crow's carefully averted gaze. She had only recently become accustomed to the changes in her body shape. Though short in arm and leg, she was shapely between and, with her long, red-brown hair and heart-shaped face, delicate nose and bright eyes, she knew that she wasn't bad-looking. Nothing compared to Asta, of course, so why worry about stripping off a couple of metres away from Crow? But she still did.

"What's cooking?" she asked, dumping herself gracelessly on the floor near the fire. She ached so much she couldn't get her limbs to behave.

"Dried smoked fish and baked beans," said Crow. "Pretty rank really but useful in emergencies."

"I don't care," said Tanith. The hollow growling in her stomach was all one with the rest of her body's complaining but now the pungent smell of the hot fish was making her light-headed with hunger.

Crow poured some of the steaming mixture onto a plate and ate his own share from the pan. The warmth from the fire and the food set Tanith's fingers and toes painfully ablaze but also had her drowsy and nodding within minutes. She was too tired for mere discomfort to keep her awake. She barely noticed and certainly made no protest as Crow led her by the hand to a grubby heap of bedding in one corner where she nestled into it like an overtired toddler. Wulfie, having gorged himself on a rabbit he had found in the woods, flopped down beside her. Crow covered them both with a stained and flattened duvet. He stamped out the fire, left the pan and plate unwashed and lay down on the other side of Wulfie. Then all three of them slept as if drugged.

14

I drag my stiff and aching body back to the town. It takes me hours; I don't know the way; I wasn't looking for landmarks on the walk up, I was so excited. All I can do is struggle to find a path down. In the end, I follow a stream that I guess must join the river which races through our little town, still restless with rapids and the memory of the mountains. Darkness falls, but I stagger on, stumbling frequently but determined to get back as fast as I can. What must the townsfolk be thinking? We have been gone so long!

It is only when I finally see the shadowy outline of the

buildings, sunk in darkness, not a light in sight, that I wonder why I have met no one looking for us, no one trying to follow our trail. I expect to see the town lit up, busy, anxious, unable to rest because of our absence. But all is quiet. Can everyone be sleeping?

Despite my exhaustion, panic sends me surging forwards. There is an unnatural silence to the town. Something is wrong – some terrible calamity has struck. Another terrible calamity. Should I knock on the first door I come to? Find out what is going on? But fear sickens me. Whatever it is, I will find out at home. It is not far now. Then I will tell my parents what happened in the mountains and they can tell the others and decide what to do. I have done all I can for now, bringing the news.

I reach the door of our cottage. The door is on the latch, as ever. I hesitate. The silence is too deep; it is eerie and unnatural. I dread to think what I will find when I push the door open but I do it anyway. Nothing will keep me from my bed any longer, however fearful.

But something does. Whatever I expected, it was not this. The room is in darkness but there is enough moonlight shed by the open door for me to see my parents, snuggled up close in their bed, sleeping peacefully, just as if their broken-bodied son was asleep as usual, tucked into his little truckle bed beside them.

But I am not. I am standing at the door, open-mouthed with astonishment, burdened with dread news which I am beginning to think is not dread news after all. I stand there, poleaxed with loss, my heart seeming to freeze within me. I know what the silence is now. The rats have gone. And so have the children. They are captive inside a mountain. And the parents are sleeping peacefully.

Tanith woke up crying, overwhelmed with grief, the numbness which had sustained her through the last few days suddenly gone in the space of a nightmare. Tears flooded her face with the gut-wrenching suddenness of vomit, spewing forth uncontrollably. Wulfie began to howl and Crow jerked awake, his heart pounding at the shock of the sudden cacophony.

"Tanith!" he shouted, springing up and scrambling over both Wulfie and her huddled form. "Tanith, hush! It's all right! You're safe here. I'm Crow – remember?"

With trembling hands, still shaken from his abrupt wakening, Crow lit a tallow candle. It burned foully but he thought it reassuring. It was daylight outside but inside the mill it was dark and dispiriting.

He squatted beside Tanith, stroking Wulfie to quieten him.

"What is it, Tanith?" he asked. "A bad dream?"

Tanith was unable to answer. She was sitting now, clutching her stomach, sobs tearing her so hard that he thought she might do herself damage. He felt helpless. He knew now that he had no immediate power to calm Tanith, unlike the many heartbroken children he had taken under his wing. Nervously, he put an arm round her shoulder and, to his surprise, she collapsed against him, huddling into his chest and soaking his sweater. He didn't know quite what to do with his free arm so he put that round her too and then waited, squatting uncomfortably on the floor, until the terrible paroxysm subsided enough for Tanith to speak.

"My grandmother," Tanith gasped, at last. "She died – just a few days ago. That's why I came to the city. I didn't want to be got by the Cratz. I...I...haven't had time to think about it."

"Did you dream about her?"

Tanith shook her head. "Not about her. Just a child – a child like me. And oh, Crow – he was so hurt! He was grieving terribly." Tears filled her eyes and began to spill over again. "I can feel it, Crow," she said, banging her chest. "I can feel it here. His pain – and mine. Together."

She wiped her face on her sleeve. Crow had nothing to offer instead so he didn't try to stop her. Heartbreak was nothing new to him – you saw it all the time in the city. Kids stumbled into his care, bewildered by the loss of parents to the sickness, to crime, to the unequal struggle for survival in such a harsh society. But it hurt him to watch Tanith crumple and to be unable to help. He tightened his arms a little around her; at least he could offer her his warmth.

"Was your grandmother ill?"

Tanith shook her head. "It wasn't the sickness, if that's what you mean. She was just very old. I was lucky to have her so long. She'd had the sickness but she survived."

"Your parents?"

"The sickness. I can hardly remember them – only the feeling that they were ill for a long, long time. First my mother and later, my father."

Suddenly Tanith became aware of Crow's arms around her. He felt her body tense.

"I…I'm all right now," she said and he took the hint and released her, standing up and flexing his legs which had begun to go dead. "I…I'm sorry. It's silly. Kids lose their parents all the time. It's no big deal. And I knew my grandmother was old. I knew she couldn't last much longer. It's just…"

"Of course it's a big deal," said Crow. "Just because it happens all the time, doesn't make it any easier. Oh, I know that's what the Cratz say – that Citz kids don't care like they do – that we're tough and hardened and all that. That's just an excuse to keep any treatment for themselves and let the Citz carry on dying. You know it isn't true. Sometimes Asta and I lose a kid. They get ill, they have an accident, sometimes they just go missing. It tears us apart every single time. Don't start believing the Cratz rubbish!"

"I don't really," said Tanith, slipping her arms round Wulfie who was trying to lick the tears from her face. "It's just…well, it's just so normal, isn't it? It doesn't seem right to make a fuss. Not when there are little tiny kids it happens to. It's not very brave."

Crow sat down, huddling against Wulfie's flank for warmth. "Tanith, you are one of the bravest people I've ever met," he said. "And the proudest. Give yourself a break. It's okay to cry when your grandmother dies, all right?"

Tanith managed a watery smile. "What about you?" she said. "What happened to your parents?"

Crow looked away and his voice suddenly lost all its warmth. "My father left me," he said. "And I left my mother a long time ago."

There was something about the rigid set of his jaw which prohibited further questions. Tanith waited, unsure what to say or do.

"It's still daylight outside," Crow said, breaking the difficult silence. "Can you sleep now?"

Tanith nodded. "Thank you, Crow," she said and snuggled back under the duvet. Wulfie burrowed under too and then thrashed around until his head popped out, making them both laugh. Crow settled himself back down to sleep and soon Tanith could hear his light breathing.

She however, stayed awake, puzzling over Crow. It was so hard to get a handle on him. Warm and caring one minute, he seemed intense and intimidating the next. And why would anyone actually choose to leave their mother? Mothers were scarce unless they were Cratz and even they sickened and sometimes died. And the depth of coldness in his voice as he had told her! It was unnerving. Should she trust him? If he was simply after Wulfie, he had missed the perfect opportunity back there on the weir. One little shove and she'd have gone. Wulfie would have struggled to rescue her without help. And he had been so kind about her dream! So why hadn't he told her what he was up to? Why the stalling? As soon as Crow was awake, she would insist on an explanation. There must be no more excuses.

15

Crow woke in the late afternoon, just as he always did. He still felt tired but he needed to get up and fish before returning to the city. Tonight he had to work and also talk to Asta about what they must do, given what Jed had told him. For months, years even, there had been rumours that missing kids ended up on the butcher's block. With so many starving on the city streets, there was a macabre logic to it. But no one had ever confirmed it before. Jed was a hardened, tough survivor. To see him tearful was proof enough for Crow. He shuddered. There had been Suki, a little girl who managed to stay plump despite their frugal life, sweet-natured but slow. And there had been Vrim, a wide-eyed innocent who had never learned when to run. Crow bit his lip, fighting back his own tears and nausea. In the rush to get Tanith and Wulfie away, he had managed to bury his horror. Now it threatened to engulf him. He knuckled his eyes and breathed in slowly. He couldn't know for sure what had happened to Suki and Vrim. There were other, better ends. And not every lost kid was never found. But he wasn't going to take any more chances. It was time to get their band of street kids out of the city. He and Asta could not protect them from a threat as evil and systematic as the one Jed had described; it was no longer fair to deny them the chance to escape to the one place Crow knew was safe, even though he had vowed he would never return there. He couldn't live with himself if another child went missing now.

Crow crept about, collecting what he needed. Wulfie raised his heavy head and cocked an ear but settled down again, content to stay with his sleeping mistress. Crow would wake her later and explain that she must wait out the night alone. The following morning, he hoped, he would be back with Asta and the kids. Then they would move on.

He was not looking forward to the talk with Asta. When she knew what he had kept hidden for so long, she would be furious. All his reasons might seem as worthless as dust in the face of the pitiful existence of the cave kids. He fingered the slender pouch at his waist in which he kept his most precious possession. He daren't tell Asta about its real power. If he did and refused to use it, he would never hear the end of it. And using it simply wasn't an option – but she would never understand why. Things were black and white for her. He envied her the straightforwardness of her thinking. For him, actions were always, at best, an uneasy grey compromise.

Crow was sitting by the river in the twilight when Tanith found him. She approached silently, hoping not to disturb the fish. Instead, still drowsy, it was Crow who was startled.

"I'm sorry," Tanith said. "I was trying to be quiet."

"It's all right," he said. "I thought you would still be asleep."

"Another bad dream," she said. "The boy was following a man with a pipe this time."

Crow flinched and looked up. Her quizzical eyes were intense, holding his gaze with a clarity he had never encountered before.

"You said you would explain why you rescued me," she said. "I want you to tell me now – before you disappear again. And there's something I need to tell you too."

"That's okay," said Crow. "I have time before I go back to the city. It was just so important to get you away quickly. Sit down."

Tanith hesitated. Crow had agreed almost too easily.

"I know," said Crow. "It's difficult. But we're safe here for a while. Honestly."

Crow told his story while he fished.

"You're not going to like this," he started. "It's terrible and it's frightening."

Tanith shrugged. "So what's new?" she said. "That's life for the Citz, isn't it?"

"But you're from the hills," said Crow. "I'm guessing it's not as bad as the city."

"It's more beautiful," she said. "And the awfulness isn't in your face all the time. But it's still hard. Especially for me, of course."

She spoke in a completely matter-of-fact way. There was no self-pity in her voice. It was just a comment about life as she lived it. Crow blushed, embarrassed again to have been so crass when they'd been struggling up from the weir.

"Well?" she said, dragging him back from his thoughts. "What's the story then?"

Crow hesitated. Faced with telling it baldly, it was hard to know where to start. It would sound extreme – ridiculous – preposterous.

"We...e...ll," he said slowly. "You know how it's really tough to get food in the city?" he said.

"It is everywhere, isn't it?" said Tanith. "Unless you're Cratz – and it's not great even for them. We were lucky, I suppose, out in the hills. We could manage – but there was never very much."

"Yes – well, in the city, people will eat anything, hunt anything, including rats. Even if you earn a bit of money, you can never afford to buy anything decent. That was the first thing I thought about Wulfie – that he would feed at least thirty hungry kids – maybe more."

Tanith gave him a very hard look. "You would have killed him for the cave kids?"

"It was my first thought, all right? And I did warn you, didn't I? In the woods?"

"I never thought you meant *you* would have killed him."

"Well, I wouldn't have done once I'd thought about it. And I haven't, have I? Anyway, my next thought was what a good hunter you could make of him."

"That's what The Boss was going to do with him," said Tanith. "He wanted me to teach Wulfie to hunt – not just for himself and for Gran and me, like he's always done – but for The Boss and Sarge and everyone else in their operation. He said he didn't care what Wulfie brought down, so long as it was meat – badgers, foxes, rats. You name it. It was disgusting. He had a huge freezer and all the equipment."

"It's worse than that, Tanith," said Crow.

"Worse?" said Tanith. "Isn't that bad enough?"

Crow swallowed. He had never put what he was going to say into words, even inside his own head. He had shrunk away from the real horror of it.

"It's kids," he said, with an effort. "The Boss and his mate were hunting kids. That's why they wanted Wulfie. He'd bring a kid down, no problem."

Tanith stared at him, stupefied.

"Kids? They were hunting *kids*? You can't mean…?"
Crow nodded.

All the colour drained from Tanith's face.

"You mean to turn into *meat*?" she gasped. "To sell to the Cratz?"

Crow nodded. "Makes sense, doesn't it?" he said. "Too many kids on the streets, lots of Cratz desperate for meat, the likes of The Boss and Sarge not too fussed about where *their* next meal ticket comes from…a big dog like Wulfie drops into their lap. Perfect!"

"I don't believe it," said Tanith. "It can't be true! How can you be sure?"

"There's been talk of it for a long time. I thought it was just rumour – urban myth. A kid goes missing here, another there – who knows? Kids go missing all the time – why would anyone suspect they're ending up on some Cratz dinner table?"

"Stop it!" cried Tanith. "Don't talk about it like that! It's sick!"

"Sorry," said Crow. He was fighting to control himself. Now that he'd actually said it, a great tide of fury and revulsion was threatening to overwhelm him. "Sorry," he said again, his voice hard and bitter. "But it's not as sick as actually doing it, is it?"

"I still don't believe it. How do you know?"

"*Why* don't you believe it?" Crow rounded on her angrily. "Because it isn't very *nice*? Asta has a book back at the caves – yes, she can read, the lucky swine – collects books wherever she can find them. It's a book about the turn of the century. Know what was happening then in Brazil? They were shooting the street kids, just because they were in the way! Bad things happen, Tanith. We all know that."

Tanith looked mulish. "People don't eat other people," she said. "Even the Cratz aren't that bad."

Crow gave a short laugh. "Don't you believe it," he said. "When people are desperate, they'll do anything. And who says the Cratz know what they're buying? Huh?"

"So tell me why you're so sure," said Tanith. "How d'you know it isn't just a rumour?"

"Remember Jed?" he asked. "The boy on the bike?"

Tanith nodded.

"It's him you've got to thank for being rescued. I was looking for you but you'd vanished. He heard where you were, heard why and told me. I just hope he's all right."

"And how did he find out? How did he *know*?"

"How did he know? Because he works for a butcher, of course. Sorry, Tanith. You may not like it but it's happening. So we've got to get you and your dog and all the kids from the caves out of the city before we lose any more."

16

Crow stood up.

"You're going?" said Tanith.

"I ought to get back. The kids will be hungry and there's a lot to do if we're going to move them out. But there was something you wanted to tell me too. Can it wait?"

"Of course. It's more important that you get back. Asta must be worried. We can talk later."

"You'll be all right here? You won't try to go anywhere?"

"You're joking! Go somewhere? With Wulfie? After what you've just told me? You think I want to end up in a freezer while my dog gets turned into a killing machine?"

Crow had his hands in his pockets and was rocking fretfully from one foot to the other, shoulders hunched, head down, his face pale and anxious in the twilight. Tanith had a strong urge to reach out and stroke the line of his cheekbones with a finger. She took a step back, shocked at her feelings, and had to grab Wulfie to steady herself.

"I think this is the safest place for you," said Crow. "If you stay put. Can you manage without a fire? You can eat cold baked beans and there are some dried apples too."

"I'll be fine. When do you think you'll be back?"

"Tomorrow evening, I hope. I ought to do another night's work before we leave. Who knows whether we'll need any money? Once we've got the kids together, it won't take long to pack up. But I don't want to move them in daylight."

"Okay," said Tanith. "I'll see you tomorrow night then. You'd better go now. I'll sort out the fishing tackle and put it away."

Still Crow hesitated. "I don't like to leave you..." he started. "What if...?"

"I told you, I'll be fine," said Tanith. "No one knows I'm here except you. Just go."

It was dark by the time Crow got back to the city and the kids were gathered round the fire that Asta had built up. He felt a sudden rush of fondness for her. Her face was animated, her curls tumbling forwards, her hands making pictures in the air as she told one of her thrilling old stories. The children were agog, eyes entranced, happily ignoring their rumbling tummies. Then Crow caught a snatch of the words.

"And the man said, 'A thousand gold coins! A thousand gold coins and I will free your town from this plague of rats!'"

Crow leaped into the circle, swinging his pole of fish.

"Crow!" Asta said, annoyed, as the children clamoured round him. "Crow, you've spoiled the story – that's not like you!"

"Sorry," said Crow, smiling into her eyes. "I don't like that story. Frightening."

Asta passed a hand across her forehead. "Where was I up to?" she said. "I've lost the thread now."

"Never mind," said Crow. "Help me with these fish. I need to talk to you."

The kids were already queuing up, pointed sticks at the ready.

"Here," said Crow, giving an extra fish to an older child. "Do one for Asta and me, please. We need to talk."

"Where's the girl? Where's Tanith?" said Asta, sounding dazed. "And the dog – Wulfie, wasn't it?"

"They're fine. I've taken them somewhere safe. They're waiting for us."

"Waiting for us? Why? What are we going to do?"

"I'm just about to tell you. Come on. Come away from the kids."

Crow took Asta by the elbow and led her away from the children before he delivered his bombshell.

"So that's what all this has been about!" said Asta. Her eyes were wide and her face white. "Why didn't you tell me?"

"I wasn't sure. Not until Jed found me. When I was first looking for Tanith, I was just working on a rumour. I didn't want to frighten you."

It wasn't the whole truth and Crow looked away, uncomfortable with himself and fearful that she would see through him. Asta had been his loyal companion and helper for three years; he felt dreadful not telling her everything but he suspected that if he did she would leave. And he needed her help right now.

Asta gave a short laugh. "Frightened? Me?"

"You don't look too good right now."

"I'm not frightened, I'm just disgusted. We have to get the kids out, Crow. Right now. But I wish you'd told me sooner." She laughed again. "I thought you fancied that girl."

Crow said nothing.

"She is pretty," Asta carried on. "Lovely hair and eyes – and a cute face. But…"

Crow cut her short. "There's something I haven't told you, Asta," he said. "You're not going to be pleased."

"Don't tell me you do fancy her?" Asta's face had flushed.

Crow shook his head. "It's nothing to do with Tanith," he said. "It's to do with me. When we met, Asta, I told you I was Cratz, right?"

Asta nodded. "A Cratz who'd run away because your dad kept beating you up…"

"Yes. Well, I lied. I'm not Cratz at all."

"You're a Citz then? But why…?"

"I guess I was trying to impress you. It's true I was having a hard time at home – but I was never a Cratz. I'm sorry, Asta."

Asta shrugged. "It doesn't matter. I always thought you knew some surprising things for a Cratz. How to gut a fish, for example. How to light a fire when everything was damp. I thought the Cratz were scared to fish because of the pollution and I couldn't imagine them ever needing to light a fire outdoors. But then I knew nothing much about them so how would I know? Why are you telling me now? Really – how you started out – it doesn't matter. It's how you are now that counts."

"The thing is, Asta," said Crow, his voice still hesitant, "I know a place where we could take the kids. A place they would be safe – out in the country. It's quite like this – it's where I came from. You see the thing is, I'm not a Citz either. I was a cave-dweller – well, sort of."

"A cave-dweller? So they really exist? But you hate caves!"

"That's because of where I came from. I hated it. I never thought I'd go back."

"Because of your dad? Did he beat you up? Was that bit true? Or was it because of the caves?"

Crow blushed. "I shouldn't have said that about my dad. He left years ago – he never laid a finger on me. The truth is, I wanted to find him. That's partly why I left home – I thought he might have come to the city. Before I met you, I searched and searched and I still keep my ear to the ground – but there's been nothing. Not in all these years."

"So why did he leave?" asked Asta.

Crow shrugged. "Stuff. It's a long story. The same stuff that made me leave in the end. But aren't you mad at me?"

"Mad at you? What for?"

"For lying. For keeping quiet about my home. Asta, I could have taken us all there any time I liked! But I wouldn't because I didn't want to go back. And I wasn't sure it was the best thing for the kids. I'm still not…"

"Is it safe?"

"Oh yes, it's safe – well, safe enough, anyway."

"Then we must take them."

"So you're not mad with me?"

"Crow, I wouldn't want to go back to the life I had before this either. I'd rather die," said Asta. "And there have always been new kids arriving in the city – you've always been needed here. You still are. But we can't stay here and run the risk of them ending up on a butcher's block – not if you're sure that's what's happening."

"As sure as I can be."

"Then we go."

"Safety isn't everything," said Crow, uncomfortably.

"It's better than nothing," said Asta. "When do we leave?"

"Tomorrow – as soon as it's dark."

"Why not now?"

"I'd feel happier with some money..."

At that moment, a large figure broke panting into the circle of children nearby.

"Where's Crow?" demanded a hoarse voice.

"Here," said Crow, striding over at once. "Jed – what are you doing here? What's wrong?"

"You've got to get these kids out," Jed gasped. "The sooner the better. I got here as quickly as I could. It's terrible news – they've got that new kid, Timbo."

Asta swayed slightly and clutched Crow's arm.

"I'm going to get him," said Crow.

"No," said Asta, her voice anguished. "You can't. He's just one kid, Crow! We have to think of the others now!"

"You'll have to get them out," said Crow. "I'll tell you the way and we'll catch you up."

"I'll go with her," said Jed, "but I think you're crazy, Crow."

"Go with her?" said Crow. "What about your job?"

"You think I'm keeping that? Haven't you listened to what I've been saying, Crow? I haven't just heard what's going on – I've seen it. I *know*. Tell me where we're going and let's go – right now."

"Fine." Quickly, Crow rapped out directions to the mill.

Then he turned to Asta. "I'll be as fast as I can," he said. "You'll explain to Tanith, won't you?"

Asta, strong, fearless Asta, had tears in her eyes. She rested her hands on Crow's shoulders and for the briefest moment, pressed her cheek against his. Then she looked up into his face.

"Take care, Crow," she said, hoarsely. "Don't be long."

He met her gaze gently. She relaxed at once and smiled.

Then Crow sprang into the circle of excited children. They clustered round him, anxious to know what was happening. He looked them firmly in the eyes. "You must do what Asta says," he told them. "Just as you always do. I'll be back as soon as I can but Timbo is lost and I must find him."

Then he hurried away.

17

I am hobbling after them, as fast as I can. Where are they all going? What's all this about? The stranger with the pipe is leading the way, playing his strange music. It is like a dance but not one that I want to join. There is something too urgent about it, too frantic. The others are leaping and skipping to its wild beat, falling over each other to get to the front of the crowd. They're laughing and chatting but as if half-crazed, not caring for bumps and bruises, scratches and grazes as they trip and fall in their haste and stub their toes on the rocky path. Where has their energy come from? This morning they were as listless and half-starved as ever. Now they look as if they could run for ever. I can't. It is all I can do to keep them in sight and if this mad chase goes on much longer, I will lose them. The last of them rounds a corner in the path, such as it is. I can hear their hectic voices but no longer the pipe. I force my aching limbs forward, swinging my stubby arms for speed but I am light-headed with hunger and effort. I know I cannot keep this up much longer.

Tanith woke, startled. After Crow had left, she had snuggled back down to sleep in the mill. She was still tired from the efforts of the last few days and there was nothing else to do but sleep. Her stomach was rumbling but it wasn't hunger that woke her. It was voices. Wulfie stuck out his muzzle from beneath the duvet, his pricked ears making it drape round his head like an old lady's scarf. Tanith would have laughed if she hadn't been so worried. Definitely voices and quite a lot of them, coming nearer. They weren't loud; in fact, as she listened closely, she could tell that they were trying to be quiet. Could they possibly be the cave kids, here earlier than expected?

Cautiously, with Wulfie glued to her side, Tanith tiptoed to the door of the mill and peered out, listening. It was still pitch-dark. If these were Crow's kids, wouldn't he be leading them? Why would they be blundering around in the dark with no clear idea of where they were going? It was more likely that a gang of drunken Cratz had strayed down to the river or that these were city bandits, returning from a night of crime. Or worse – and Tanith shivered at the thought – a gang of hunters, the sort The Boss had described.

Tanith shrank back into the doorway, her eyes peeled for any movement close by, desperate to know what was going on. It had been quiet for a while; perhaps whoever it was had passed by. But it didn't feel like they had. Wulfie was still tense and alert and Tanith felt sure she was not alone.

Then, from the undergrowth above the mill, Tanith heard a quite unmistakeable voice, small and tired.

"Are we there yet?"

Tanith took a risk, a cruel one which she hated doing. Deliberately, she trod on Wulfie's paw. He yelped loudly.

"Sorry, sorry," she mouthed, hugging him. "I couldn't think of anything else."

"A dog!" said a child, somewhere above her in the darkness. "Down there! A dog!"

And then came a voice she recognized. "This way, Jed," said Asta. "I think that was Wulfie!"

At that Tanith stepped out into the yard.

"Asta!" she called. "Crow! Where are you? I'm down here."

Then the bushes came alive with excited chattering and strenuous shushing too. Moments later, the kids spilled into the yard.

"In here!" said Tanith. "Quickly! And be quiet!"

She ushered them all in, Asta and Jed bringing up the rear.

"I'll find a light," Tanith said, stumbling across to the bed.

"Don't bother," said Asta. "It would be a waste. We've walked all this way in the dark. We don't need a light now. Quick, kids – find a space to lie down. This is where we're staying for a while."

"But where's Crow?" asked Tanith. "And why have you come now? Crow said to expect you tomorrow evening."

"We've had a bad shock," said Jed. "It made us want to get out fast. Your friend The Boss has got Timbo."

"Timbo?" Tanith felt as if icy fingers had grasped her guts. She had a sudden horrific vision of that warm little hand, severed on a butcher's block.

"Yes, Timbo," said Asta. "You met him. Clueless. Crow would have kept close by him for a couple of days if he hadn't been looking for you."

"That's not my fault!" said Tanith, furious.

"Of course it isn't," said Jed. "Asta didn't mean it was. We're all just tired and anxious about Timbo. And about Crow."

"About Crow?" echoed Tanith.

"He's gone looking for Timbo, of course," said Asta. "What did you expect?"

Crow found Jed's abandoned bike on the cusp of the sandstone ledge which skirted the caves and tunnels. He leaped astride it, reckoning that Jed wouldn't need it any more. He wasn't used to cycling but was fit and strong and soon got into the rhythm, hurtling through the dark city by back routes, hoping he wouldn't attract much notice. If any of The Boss's cronies recognized him, he would have a reception committee awaiting him at the garages. With one hand, he checked his pockets. Matches. Hip flask, full he was sure. He'd checked it only recently. Good. He had a knife at his waist and his surviving firestaff slung across his back. That would have to do. If The Boss and Sarge had guns he was in trouble, but he doubted that they did. The police were ruthless in carrying out the gun law. Only they carried firearms. Possession meant death. Immediate, ruthless, no questions asked. It was an effective measure, cocooning the Cratz from the more murderous element of the Citz.

It took Crow less time than he had thought to find the bridge over the canal where Jed had dumped Tanith but now the long hill stretched ahead of him. Crow got off and pushed, whistling innocently, a butcher boy on his way home from a hard day's work. Or even, he thought suddenly, a butcher boy making a less than innocent visit to the garages. Perhaps that was his entrée. Well, for want of a better one, it would do. It should get him through the gate at least. He knew the name of Jed's employer. That might prove useful.

But when Crow reached the yard, the gates were open. He peered inside, alert, on his guard. There was the beaten-up van which Sarge had used to chase them. The metal door of Tanith's prison was half-open. From inside,

Crow could hear voices. Right, so he could pretend he was Jed, come to collect an order or something – but what then? He had no idea what his next move could be. He looked at the van. It had no windows except in the front, a typical delivery van. Supposing, just supposing, Timbo was still inside?

Crow crept forwards and crouched down by the back doors, then reached his hand underneath. Yes, it was hot. The van must have only recently pulled up. Maybe Timbo was still in there? But how could he find out?

Crow pressed his ear to the side of the van and waited.

Nothing. He tried the doors. Locked, of course. Despite the freezing night air, Crow was breaking out in a sweat. He was wasting time but he couldn't think what else to do. Then, just as he was giving up hope, the metal against his cheek vibrated. And again. Something was definitely moving. The van rocked slightly and Crow thought he heard a moan. Right. Someone was in there and it could be Timbo. He'd just have to take a chance.

Crow peered through the driver's window. Good. There was no barrier between the front seats and the storage area. If he could get into the front, he could get into the back. All he had to do was smash a window. But he couldn't break glass silently and as soon as he made a noise, whoever was in the garage would be in the yard.

He needed Asta with her lock-picking skills. Stupid! Jed could have led the kids to the mill. Crow ground his teeth in fury at himself – why, oh why hadn't he thought about *locks*? He'd panicked and now look at the mess he was in, armed with only a firestaff and his knife.

But a desperate plan was unfolding in his mind and the sooner he put it into action, the better. Hidden by the bulk of the van, he pulled out his hip flask and soaked the wicks of his firestaff with paraffin. Then he laid it on the ground and lit both ends. He would have to be quick. His wicks wouldn't burn for ever.

There was all sorts of tat lying around the yard. Crow picked up a hunk of rusted metal, wrapped it in his jacket and smashed the driver's window. He reached down, opened the door and scrambled into the back, where sure enough, bound and gagged, lay Timbo. Already Crow could hear shouts and movement from outside; there was no time to free the kid now. He threw himself back over the driver's seat and half-fell out of the van, just in time to snatch up his firestaff, get his balance and hurl himself at Sarge.

Sarge was thrown by the suddenness of the attack and crumpled back against the wall of the yard. Crow pressed his advantage, bringing his staff up against the man's throat, forcing his neck back to breaking point. He had done this before; he never enjoyed it, it was never something he sought but there had been times when it had been the only way to survive. Sarge was clawing at the staff, his eyes bulging, when The Boss leaped on Crow from behind. But Crow had been expecting him. He swung the staff round, sending Sarge reeling with a glancing, burning blow to the head and brought up the other end in

The Boss's face. The Boss cringed away from him with an animal howl, his hands flying to cover his burned cheek and beat at his smouldering hair. Sarge, gagging for air, had managed to recover himself and was staggering forwards, but quailed at the site of Crow, whirling his staff in a dizzying figure of eight.

Crow wanted to leave it at that. If he could have crawled into the van, released Timbo and legged it, he would have done, but he knew that the moment he put down the staff, he was dead.

"You can let me get that kid out or—" he shouted but Sarge didn't give him chance to finish. With a croak that was meant to be a roar, he hurled himself forwards, oblivious to Crow's ring of fire, going for his ankles. Crow didn't hesitate. He leaped aside and Sarge fell. Then he stood on him and calmly set light to his jacket.

Only then did he dare drop the firestaff, spring back into the van, slit Timbo's bonds and shove him mercilessly out into the yard.

"Run!" he shrieked at the quaking child. "Run down the hill to the canal! Wait by the bridge!"

He glanced round the yard. No sign of the man whose face he'd burned. Crow fleetingly registered disgust. Doubtless he'd gone for water for his burn, leaving Sarge to his fate. Crow snatched up his own jacket again and hurled it on top of the screaming man who, to his relief, had stayed where he had fallen. He pressed down hard with his hands and then rolled Sarge over, extinguishing the flames almost as quickly as he'd lit them.

"You're not dead," he spat in the man's face. "That'll have barely scorched you. But if you follow me, it'll be worse – believe me!"

Sarge's ghastly face sagged in front of him, lit up by the flame of the burning staff. The man looked incapable of speech, let alone following Crow.

Crow squeezed the wicks dead between his boots, then ran, not waiting to sling his staff across his back but hurtling down the hill on Jed's bike, with it balanced across the handlebars.

At the bridge, he found Timbo, collapsed against it, utterly winded.

"Did you kill them?" he croaked, his eyes appalled.

Crow shook his head. "I don't want to stoop to their level," he said. "But we're not safe yet. Come on – we have to go."

"Crow, I can't," whimpered Timbo. "I just can't."

"Oh yes you can," insisted Crow, fixing him with a steely gaze.

Then he took out the tiny pipe that hid at his waist and put it to his lips.

18

Crow and Timbo had just crossed the weir when Crow heard something up ahead. Immediately, he tucked his pipe into its pouch and grabbed Timbo by the collar as he slumped. Gently, he let him collapse onto the floor and then swung round his firestaff, barring the path and standing astride Timbo's body. There was time for nothing else and, in any case, he had used all his paraffin.

He listened carefully. It was certainly more than one person approaching. A bunch of hunters probably. With luck, they would have no interest in him and Timbo. He could detect at least two sets of footfalls, possibly three. But at least one of the owners was old or lame; they walked awkwardly, they...

"Tanith!"

Wulfie bounded forward, almost knocking Crow over in his enthusiasm, unsure whether to jump up and lick him or snuffle at the child who lay on the floor.

"Crow!" Tanith stood stock-still in the middle of the path, beaming her relief. "I thought we'd come and look for you, I was so worried."

"You shouldn't have been," said Crow, grinning nonetheless, "but I'm very glad to see you. Poor Timbo is done in."

"We can put him on Wulfie," said Tanith. "He's only little. If you hold him steady, he'll be all right. Did you have to carry him far?"

"Oh...uh...no, not far," said Crow, stooping over Timbo to hide the lie. "Come on, Timbo – wake up for me. Not far now, all right?"

"We'd better hurry," said Tanith, "and be quiet. I've been keeping watch and there were hunters around earlier; I thought they might be after us."

Crow helped Timbo onto Wulfie's back where he could barely hold himself upright. His head lolled forwards and he seemed incapable of gripping with his legs.

"Let's go," said Crow. "He's had a terrible experience. We need to get him somewhere where he can sleep."

Tanith looked at the child uneasily. There was a strange

blankness about his face that was unnerving.

"He looks like he's in a trance," she said as they moved off, Crow holding Timbo steady.

"It's probably shock," said Crow. "I found him bound and gagged in the back of that van at the garage. And then…well, I'll tell you later. Better be quiet here."

Shock? thought Tanith. *No, that isn't it.* The child seemed almost comatose. He wasn't just tired and he wasn't just shocked, she was sure of that. There was something that Crow wasn't telling her.

At the mill, they found Asta doling out tiny portions of cold baked beans, a spoonful at a time, straight into a line of hungry mouths. As soon as Crow walked in, the queue broke up, the kids crowding round Crow excitedly.

"Stand back," he said, sternly. "You're not giving Timbo space to breathe." Gently, he lifted the child down from Wulfie, laid him on the simple bed and covered him with the duvet.

"He needs to sleep," he told Asta, who had laid aside the beans and spoon to join the throng clustered about Crow.

"We were so worried," said Asta, her eyes glued to Crow's face. "What happened? Have you been followed?"

He shook his head. "I'll tell you later. Let's get these kids fed first."

Tanith stood back, wondering. The kids must be starving. Food was always a priority. They had scarcely been able to contain their impatience as they queued. There had been mutterings about some kids getting bigger spoonfuls than others. And yet, the moment they saw Crow, they had flocked to his side. No one had asked about Timbo; he'd been almost knocked off Wulfie in the rush. All right, so Crow was the one leading them out of the city but that didn't quite explain it – not the utter devotion he inspired.

He was attractive – very attractive. Asta obviously felt it too. But at the same time, he was disquieting and difficult.

Tanith had been thinking of telling him her grandmother's story. She longed to share it with someone she could trust – and surely you had to trust someone who saved your life – twice? But something was holding her back now – her troubling dreams, the nature of her story, these nagging doubts about him. She was irritated with herself – why couldn't she work him out? Why was she drawn to him one minute and suspicious of him the next? Maybe he was the last person to whom she should tell her grandmother's story? She would wait, she would watch – surely soon she must see.

It was well into the morning before Crow allowed them to leave. At first they had thought to wait till nightfall but in the end they decided to travel by daylight. Few people ventured into the wilder countryside except for hunters, and they tended to work in the dark. Crow felt that anyone they did happen to meet would steer well clear of such a rabble of riff-raff – and if news of their journey got back to the city, at least they would have a hefty headstart.

"Why would anyone bother anyway?" said Jed, bitterly. "There are plenty more kids where these came from. It'd be an awful lot of hassle just to catch a big dog."

"I'm not so sure," said Tanith, her arm wrapped round Wulfie protectively. "We're not very far from the city – and those men really wanted my dog."

"I just wish we could get more kids out," said Jed. "Just think – if we were a bit smaller and less streetwise, any one of us could have ended up in that freezer."

"I nearly did," muttered Tanith.

"Well, it's no good worrying about it," said Asta. "If we could get all the kids out of the city, we would. But we can't. We can only do our best."

Crow stood up suddenly and turned away. The kids broke up into excited groups. Now that the decision had been made they couldn't wait to leave, but Asta insisted that they let Timbo sleep for a couple of hours longer.

Tanith followed Crow. He was cramming his store of dried fish into a battered backpack, as if he was killing it all over again.

"What's up?" Tanith asked.

Crow gave a snort of laughter. "What's up? Isn't it obvious," he said.

Tanith sighed. "I meant about what Asta said. About getting them all out. She's right, Crow. You can only do your best. We can't save all of them – it would be impossible!"

"Who says it would?" snapped Crow, his face flushing angrily. "You? What would you know about it exactly?"

Tanith held up her hands and backed away. "Hey, slow down!" she said. "I could see you were upset, that's all."

"Well, aren't you? It's not very nice, is it? What's happening back there?"

"Okay, okay, sorry I spoke. I was interfering. Forget it."

"Right," said Crow, fastening the bag buckles. "Fine by me."

"Right," said Tanith. But she wasn't going to forget it. Far from it. She had every intention of remembering their strange conversation until she found out exactly what was bothering Crow so much.

They travelled slowly, unwilling to use anything but the most obscure paths, the little ones struggling where brittle bramble stems entwined the way or they had to balance close to the riverbank. For the first time, Tanith was glad it was winter; the route would have been impassable later in the year.

At last they escaped the lower reaches of the river and their path began to climb. There was no longer any cover and Tanith winced as she saw how conspicuous the kids were, strung out across the bare wintry fields. The younger ones were tiring and took it in turns to ride on Wulfie. Crow strode ahead, leading the way, his long black hair streaming in the biting wind, his firestaff suddenly a walking stick. The oldest and liveliest of the children were battling to keep up with him. Timbo clung to his free hand.

Asta, a child hanging on to her either side, turned to Tanith.

"He could be the Pied Piper," she said, fondly.

"The who?" said Tanith.

"Oh, it's an old story," said Asta. "German, I think. Something about this man who played his pipe to rid a town of rats – and then, when they had gone, the citizens refused to pay. So he played again and all the children followed him. They never came back. Crow doesn't like the story – he always stops me telling it. He thinks it will frighten the children because he's so good at playing the pipe."

"Right," said Tanith. "I see." She reached out a hand to Wulfie, plodding faithfully beside her, a child balanced on his back. She had an unpleasant sensation that the whole hill was shifting and that she was going to go hurtling to the bottom.

"Are you all right?" said Asta. "You look ill. I guess this is a bit much for you."

"I'm fine," said Tanith. "Just a bit tired. Aren't you?"

But really, she wasn't fine at all. She was thinking about her grandmother's story. And her recent unnerving dreams. And the state that Timbo had been in that morning. And the slender pouch at Crow's belt. Now she was letting him lead a pack of children up into the hills because he claimed they were all going to be butchered. With a horrible feeling of nausea, she realized that she only had his word for it. The Boss had never mentioned using Wulfie to hunt children. Had he?

Should she tell someone? Asta? She would never believe anything suspicious about Crow; the bond between them was obvious. Jed? Jed was supposed to know the truth but what reason was there to trust him? Okay, so they had all helped to rescue her but so what? Whatever else might be going on, her dog was a hot property. And then there was the oddness of Crow's penetrating gaze. In the woods that first time, there had been that strange warm wooziness when she had stared up into his eyes. She recalled his sharp look at the caves and her sudden dizziness. And before they had crossed the weir. "You can do this," he had said, locking eyes with her, holding her chin. She had shaken herself free, hating the sensation that he was scouring her mind. It was as if he had been trying to hypnotize her – and who would try unless they expected to succeed? Why had it taken her till now to realize? But it had been Timbo's trance-like state this morning that had really made her suspicious. So where did that leave Asta and Jed? Were they acting freely or did Crow have some uncanny power over them too? Whatever. There was no point in sharing her worries with them.

The child riding Wulfie suddenly lolled against her, asleep where she sat. Tanith gave her a little shake.

"Sorry, sweetheart," she said. "You have to hold on."

Wulfie's head turned at the sound of her voice. Wulfie liked Crow. Tanith had never known Wulfie to be wrong about a person – but maybe he was in thrall to Crow too? It was so confusing and anyway, what could she do? Turn tail and run back to the city? What would happen to the children then? And she certainly had no chance of persuading them not to follow their leader. All she could do was plod on and see what happened. At least she had been more or less immune to Crow's power, whatever it was, so far. But then she thought of the child in her grandmother's story. He'd been immune to what had happened too and where had that got him?

19

They have gone! The path is empty. I am alone, abandoned, here in this mountain wilderness and I have no idea what to do. How can they have vanished? There were scores of them a moment ago, skipping and chattering as if it were a fair day. I crane my eyes for a flicker of movement, strain my ears for a hint of sound. Nothing. Am I mad? Am I dreaming? I pinch myself and it hurts but then my whole body hurts, it is so tired from the merry dance we have all been led. All? There is only me here, alone on the path and this is no dream because when I dream my aches and pains vanish and I swing my legs with the abandon of the children I envy.

Then I spot it. A snake-like flash of colour, carelessly lost, gracing a wayside boulder. I hobble forwards and tentatively pick up the braided wool belt, half-wondering if I will suddenly be spirited away. The wool is warm; it has not long since left its owner's body. I hunt wildly – the opening of a cave, a gully, a ravine! There must be one here somewhere.

It is not so hard to find. A stone's throw from the belt rises a narrow cleft in the mountain wall, a squeeze for a well-grown man but no challenge to a runt of a child. I slide in sideways and at once I can hear them again, ahead of me down a tempting tunnel, their voices still eager and hectic. I follow them until, suddenly, they are quiet – unnaturally quiet. Utterly silent. Fear lends me speed and I hurry along, bouncing off the walls in my haste, until I see what has robbed them of their voices.

I am appalled.

Tanith woke up, cold and aching. After her few nights in the city, the huge silence of the moorland at night had crept into her dreams and unsettled her. She was cold because she wasn't huddled against Wulfie, merely head to head with him. She had given place to as many of the littlest kids as could get close. They loved his warmth, his fur and his velvety ears and had arranged themselves along his flanks like demanding piglets. Sighing, he had settled down among them, his nose on his paws, the picture of long-suffering patience. Now, sensing Tanith's wakefulness, he licked her face.

Tanith sat up to rub her aching joints and stretch her stiff limbs. In pain, ill at ease and lonely, it was hard to resist the urge to cry for her dead grandmother. It hurt so much it was as if an iron-clad fist had punched a hole in her ribs. Right now she missed her grandmother's big, strong hands, weather-worn and hard but blissfully soothing when she massaged Tanith's body with her comforting oils.

Clumsily, Tanith got to her feet. A little slow walking might help, a few gentle stretches.

"Tanith?"

It was Crow.

Tanith turned abruptly, stifling her gasp of alarm. Crow was sitting a short distance away, propped against a boulder, an elvish silhouette in the moonlight.

"Couldn't you sleep?" whispered Tanith, stumbling over to him.

"No – and then I thought I'd better keep watch," he said, keeping his voice low. "You look uncomfortable."

Tanith grimaced. "It's the cold," she said. "My joints don't like it and my limbs stiffen up. It's bad – too much time outdoors. I'm afraid I might slow you down tomorrow."

Crow nodded. "You usually walk better," he said.

"I know. If my grandmother was still here, she would massage me – but she isn't, so that's that."

Crow considered for a moment. "I could have a go," he said. "It can't be that hard, can it? I mean, I've nothing else to do and I can't sleep. What d'you think? Would it do any harm?"

Tanith was startled. She looked at him warily, all kinds of conflicting feelings suddenly overloading her mind. Right then, she would give almost anything for someone to rub her sore, stiff body – but Crow? This person whom she suspected had mind powers she didn't understand and about whom she had such dark, unsettling doubts? Would it be safe? At the same time, the thought of his touch sent such a quiver of excitement through her that she almost gasped.

"Err...I...d...don't know," she said. "No, I don't think it would do any harm."

"Sit down, then," he said. "Where should I start? Your shoulders?"

"Err...it's my hips and knees really," said Tanith.

"Knees then. Would you be better lying down?"

Slowly, awkwardly, more clumsily than ever, Tanith sat.

"Here, lie back on my jacket," said Crow, spreading it behind her.

"You'll get cold," she said.

"Don't worry, I'll be fine," he replied, smiling at her. He put his hands either side of her right knee and rotated them gently. "Here?" he said. "Is that right? Tell me if I'm hurting you."

He was but Tanith didn't care. Massage always hurt her

at first, she was used to that. Now, however, the pain was overridden by the crazy, searing excitement that was creeping up her body.

You mustn't feel like this, she told herself. *You don't trust him. You don't really know him. Stop him, stop him now!*

But she couldn't bear to.

"Enough?" he said, pausing. "Is it helping? Hips now?" He seemed slightly breathless with the effort.

Tell him to stop, Tanith told herself. *This is mad. You mustn't let him carry on!*

Quickly, before she could change her mind, she reached out and grabbed his hands.

"Stop it, Crow!" she said.

"What? Did I hurt you?"

Their eyes met.

"No…" Tanith breathed.

Then, suddenly, Crow was leaning forwards and Tanith was reaching up to wrap her arms around him.

Don't do this, hammered a little voice inside Tanith's head but she couldn't stop herself. Her lips were softening to meet his…

"Crow!" It was Asta.

Crow sprang back as if torched.

"What?" he snapped.

"*What?* What are you doing to Tanith, that's what!"

"Massage," said Crow. "Her joints have got sore with the cold. Is there a problem with that?"

Even though they were a couple of metres apart, Tanith

saw the way Crow sought Asta's eyes and locked them with his.

Asta wilted. "No, of course not," she said, mildly. "You'd better carry on."

But Tanith scrambled away. "It's all right," she said, coldly. "He'd finished anyway."

"Tanith, I…" Crow began.

"No," said Tanith. "Really. I'm fine now. We're finished."

Just as on the previous day, Crow led the way and Tanith brought up the rear, but she could still feel the atmosphere between them. Everyone else seemed uncomfortable too, the kids snappish and whining, Jed sunk into a silent plod and Asta unusually waspish with her small companions.

We're all tired, thought Tanith. *And hungry. That's all it is.* Certainly the almost carnival air of the adventure had disappeared. The hills, bald and bleak, stretched far into the distance and no one seemed to have the guts to ask how much further they had to go. Some of the kids had blisters, others staggered on as if they could barely put one foot in front of the other. It was becoming harder and harder to persuade the little ones to clamber off Wulfie when they had finished their turn.

But in her heart, Tanith knew the depression that had settled on the group wasn't as simple as that. Crow's lean face was hard and forbidding this morning, his body taut with suppressed feeling. He had barely spoken over the cooking and eating of the rabbits Wulfie had caught and had scolded them all into an uncomfortably hasty departure.

I should talk to him, she thought. *Find out the truth*. But she shied away from that, infuriated by the cavalier way he had suppressed Asta and afraid, not only of whatever strange powers he had, but of her own feelings. She plodded on silently, gritting her teeth against the pain in her hips, wishing he really had finished the massage.

They had been walking all morning and some, at least, were growing faint with hunger when Wulfie suddenly stood stock-still, ears flattened back, muzzle up, nose twitching as he stared back the way they had come. His growl was strong, harsh and threatening. The kid on his back looked at Tanith anxiously.

"Wulfie's rumbling," he said. "I can feel him."

"Crow!" shouted Tanith. "Wait! Something's wrong. Wulfie's growling!"

They had been climbing hard and the path behind them was obscured by a fold in the hill but at that moment, a man appeared round it, swiftly followed by another and a woman. They were advancing quickly, calm and efficient in their stride, fit and ready for anything the countryside could throw at them.

"Hunters!" yelled Tanith. "Run!"

She might as well have asked the boulders to walk. The children were beyond running. Some tried but it was as much as they could do to hobble a little quicker. The female hunter wouldn't need the gun she carried quite openly.

A quick sprint and she could simply knock some heads together.

Tanith snatched the little kid who was still clinging onto Wulfie and set him on his feet.

"Go to Crow," she told him. "Go as fast you can! Wulfie and I will hold them off!"

She had no idea whether that was possible but she couldn't think what else to do. Above her, she could hear Asta and Jed calling to the kids, herding them together, dragging and carrying them up the hill.

She grabbed Wulfie's collar and turned to face the three hunters who had caught up with her and stopped, forming a half-circle.

The woman levelled the gun at Tanith.

"Useful dog," she said, curtly. "Give him up or I'll shoot."

Don't panic, Tanith told herself. *Stay calm. Play for time.*

"If you want the dog, you'll have to take me too," she said. "He'll only listen to me."

Above her, drifting down the hillside, she suddenly, bizarrely, became aware of music – very faint, barely audible, but music, nonetheless. It was intoxicating, muddying her thoughts, making her want to turn and seek it out. Tanith shook her head hard. She had to focus on these hunters; if she didn't, she would lose her dog.

But the hunters were confused too. They were staring upwards, mouths hanging open, faces agape. Tanith chanced the briefest of glimpses behind her, saw what had distracted the hunters and took her opportunity. She flung

141

herself at the woman's ankles, trying to bring her down, praying that Wulfie would get the message that these were attackers.

He did. With one massive bound, Wulfie floored the woman, who split her head on a rock as she fell. Tanith snatched up the gun before the men had registered what was happening. Then, holding it steady, praying that they didn't realize she had never even seen a gun close-up, let alone used one, she backed away, Wulfie running and snapping at her side.

"Come any closer," she said, "and I'll shoot!"

One of the men was bending over the woman.

"Leave her!" he shouted to the other man who was hesitating. "You saw what happened to them kids. One minute they could hardly crawl; the next they were off like rabbits! And Cass is hardly breathing. I don't like this – this is spooky – let's get out of here!"

Clumsily, he hoisted the woman's limp form over his shoulders and set off back down the hill. His companion still hesitated so Tanith, a good twenty metres away now, waved the gun, and shouted.

"I mean it," she said. "Follow me and I'll shoot!"

The man believed her. He fled.

Only then did Tanith turn to see what was happening to the children above her.

The music had stopped. The hillside was empty.

20

Crow couldn't believe it when he heard Tanith's warning cry. They were so close – surely they could make it without...? But the moment he saw the gun, he knew he had no choice. The littlest kids were burned out, barely able to set one foot in front of the other. He had been confident that they would get there, albeit slowly, but there was no way they could suddenly run without his help.

There was no time to waste. He ripped open the slender pouch at his waist, set the pipe to his lips, and played the most powerful and energizing tune he knew.

The effect was instantaneous. Tiny children who had been tearful with tiredness, bigger kids who had been whining with weariness, were suddenly racing up the hill as fast as hares with hounds on their tails. They weren't laughing and calling to each other – no, his music had too much urgency for that – it was more of a race to the finish line. He led the way, running himself the last few metres to the bottom of the gritstone edge which loomed above them.

Seconds later, all the kids were bunched about him, hidden behind a vast outcrop of rock. At once Crow began to play a different tune. Then he slid his way through a slim gash, barely noticeable to the uninitiated.

No one hesitated. Powered by the music, they simply followed Crow into the hillside as unquestioningly as sheep running into a fold. Seconds later they emerged, gasping with awe in a well-hewn tunnel, lit with torches in wall sconces and sloping gently downwards. Their aches and pains forgotten, the kids hurried after Crow, whose pipe was back in its pouch.

They rounded a corner and suddenly faced pitch-darkness.

"Crow?" said Asta. "What's going on?"

"It's all right," said Crow, his voice ringing out so that everyone could hear. "My people have heard us coming and have put out the torches. Don't worry. No human could have got through our entrance unaided. They'll know that one of us is with you. The darkness is just a precaution."

"What do you mean, 'no human'?" demanded Asta.

"Who are these people? Aren't they just like you?"

"Ssh," said Crow. "Wait."

A sudden voice startled them.

"Who are you?" it boomed in the confined space. "Identify yourselves."

For reply, Crow played a brief snatch of music, energetic and strong.

There was an audible gasp.

"Crow?" said the voice. "Is that you?"

Crow played his tune again.

Instantly, a light was struck and a man, a torch in his hand, appeared out of the gloom. "Lamps!" he rapped and immediately wall sconces were lit high above their heads. Beyond the children, alert and at the ready, stood a bank of bowmen. Above them, poised on a gallery which spanned an intricately wrought set of gates, waited more archers.

Crow stepped forwards and bowed to the man who stood weaponless before the gates but with a pipe in his hand.

"Tell the Pied Piper that Crow has sent these children," he said. "Now I'm sorry but I must go."

Immediately, he turned and would have run back up the tunnel but for a concerted wail from the kids.

"Where are you going?" Asta cried. "You can't just leave us here!"

"Don't worry," said Crow. "You'll be safe, I promise. But I must find Tanith and Wulfie."

"No!" said Asta, catching at his arm. "Don't just—"

Crow took Asta's hands and drew her close to him. He met her eyes firmly. "I'll be back, Asta, I promise," he murmured. "But I can't leave Tanith out there alone with those hunters. You understand that, don't you?"

Then he released her and turned to Jed, holding his gaze for a moment before clapping him on the back in farewell.

Jed gave him a friendly shove. "Get going, Crow," he said. "We'll be all right now."

"Of course," said Asta, suddenly bright and businesslike. "Come on, children, let's see what's inside these gates. Isn't this an adventure?"

The man with the pipe bowed graciously, signalled to the bowmen to put down their weapons, then opened the gates and led the way deeper into the hillside.

At first, Tanith wouldn't believe it. Despite her uneasy suspicions, faced with the evidence of their truth, she wanted a way out. Her last glimpse of the kids had caught them racing after Crow, their aches and pains and weariness forgotten. Now they had vanished.

"Wulfie," she cried. "Find Crow."

But Wulfie was bewildered, clearly as confused by the complete disappearance of his friends as she was. He ran in increasingly large circles, whimpering.

Tanith began stumbling up the hill again, shouting for Crow, her voice harsh with anguish and fury. "Crow! Crow! Where are you?"

Above her head and stretching out to her right ran a dark boulder wall, the hard, wind-carved lip of an escarpment. She knew it, had been familiar with its bulk all her life, at a distance. It was one of the famous gritstone edges of the landscape and the thought that they were climbing towards it had comforted her the day before. Now she looked along its length and despaired. Where, in this mass of grotesquely carved boulders, hidden fissures and secret crannies, could Crow have found shelter for the kids? For that was what she told herself he must have done. Despite her dreams, despite her grandmother's story, despite her suspicions, her mind rebelled at the thought of anything more mysterious. Crow had said he knew a place where he could take the children; they must have been nearer than she guessed. But she had never expected to be left behind.

She was too exhausted and disheartened to go any further. Every swing of her legs over the rough, rock-strewn ground was misery. She slumped down on a convenient boulder, wiped the tears from her face, grated by the bitter wind, and buried her head in her hands. Wulfie, whining, sat beside her. He rested his big muzzle on her shoulder and nuzzled her ear. She turned her face and let him lick her cheek, though it stung.

"What now, Wulfie?" she said. "What are we going to do now?"

Wulfie shuddered and placed a paw on Tanith's lap. She wrapped her arms round him and buried her face in his neck, reassured as ever by his steadiness and warmth.

Hope flickered in her breast – at least Wulfie had stayed with her and fought off the hunters. He hadn't followed Crow.

But it was only a tiny flicker. The cruel fact was that the boy who had seemed about to kiss her only a few hours ago, had now abandoned her in this wilderness, exhausted, starving, cold and in pain.

And why not? He had Asta after all. Why would he want a runt of a thing like her, when it was clear he could have virtually any girl he looked at? She had been but a brief novelty among the many.

But one thing didn't make sense. Abandon her, yes – why not? But Wulfie? Why leave him free to be captured and trained to kill? Did Crow really care so little about the other city kids?

Tanith sighed wearily. One thing was clear. It was Wulfie and her again, alone in the countryside. What next? She could not go back to the city. The strands of her grandmother's story were tangled with Crow's and had brought her here. There was nothing to be gained by retracing her steps. The way forward was hidden on this hillside somewhere. Her task was to find it. The challenge was to survive while doing so. And that was not going to be easy.

The wind had dropped but it was still intensely cold and the sky was leaden. Tanith had lived in these hills all her life; she knew when snow was on the way. The first priority was to find some shelter.

"Up we get, Wulfie," said Tanith, groaning, and resting all her weight on his shoulders, she hauled herself to her feet. She was stiffer and more unsteady than ever so she inched her way along the bottom of the rock face, using it for support, placing her feet with the utmost care. Somewhere along this edge, Crow had hidden the children away. If she couldn't solve that mystery, at least she might come upon a nook big and sheltered enough to escape the storm. Snowflakes, the tiny persistent kind, were already beginning to fall. It wouldn't be long, Tanith guessed, till they built up to a serious white-out. Wulfie was nosing ahead of her eagerly but how could he know what to look for? All too aware of the darkening landscape, Tanith was struggling to keep from panicking.

"Tanith! Tanith!"

She could just hear her name on the wind. Crow! He hadn't abandoned her after all.

"Here!" Tanith yelled, all her doubts and suspicions immediately overridden by a surge of joy. "Over here! We're over here!"

She peered along the edge but she couldn't see anyone. From a distance, the edge appeared to be a smooth shallow arc but in fact boulders spilled out higgledy-piggledy, blocking all but the few metres ahead. Crow could be just round the next rocky spur.

He wasn't, but she could still hear him calling. She battled on, dizzied now by the swirling snowflakes, stopping frequently to dash them from her eyelashes. It was hard to tell if Crow's voice was getting closer; she could only pray that he hadn't set off along the edge in the opposite direction to her.

Then, suddenly, just when she was convinced that she had slipped into a nightmare and was dreaming his voice, she turned and there he was, clambering towards her, as hampered by the weather as she.

The hope of rescue was too much for Tanith. She swayed slightly, unable to take another step. She simply waited, her eyes fixed on Crow, desperate not to lose him in the thickening storm. Wulfie, almost demented with excitement, ran backwards and forwards between them, clearly bewildered by Tanith's refusal to budge.

Then Crow was just a couple of paces away and Tanith almost fell forwards into his outstretched arms. He gathered her to him, holding her tight, kissing her hair and her upturned face.

"I thought I'd lost you," he said. "I thought you would go. And when I saw that it was snowing…"

"I thought you'd left me deliberately," said Tanith. "I couldn't work it out… I still can't…"

"I can explain," said Crow. "I must explain. But first we have to get out of this weather. Come on. Get on my back."

"I can manage," said Tanith. "I'm okay."

Crow didn't argue or try to force her; he just led the way, offering a steadying hand occasionally, as Tanith clawed her way after him, mind-managing her pain.

At last Crow found what he was looking for, a deep recess in the gritstone, a slab of rock balanced slantwise above it.

"In here," he shouted above the screaming wind, and the three of them blundered in, Tanith and Crow wiping snow from their raw faces, stamping and shaking to get the worst of it off. Crow led them as far back as possible and they huddled together, Wulfie slumped across them, all soaked but almost cosy with relief and their shared body heat. Through the narrow entry to their sanctuary they could see that the afternoon had sunk into wintry gloom, light and landscape obliterated by the whirling snow.

Tanith found that she was leaning back against Crow's chest and that he had one arm wrapped around her shoulder. She thought his cheek was resting against the top of her head. Was that what he wanted or was it simply that they had so little space? She didn't move, though, and didn't suggest that he did. She felt warm and safe and happier than she had done for days.

"All right," she said, relaxing back and hoping for the best. "Explain. Where are the kids? What have you done with them?"

Crow was silent.

"Well?" said Tanith. "Don't you think...? Crow?"

Crow's breathing was warm and steady against her hair. The hand draped over her shoulder was limp. He had fallen asleep.

21

Horror overwhelms me, horror at what I have seen and horror at my own cowardice in fleeing. But I don't stop. Behind me, I can hear voices, running footsteps. My noisy, blundering escape has attracted attention. Along the tunnel, delicate intoxicating music is drifting but it has no power over me. To make certain I ram my fingers in my ears, bashing my elbows on the rough walls and staggering worse than ever. But I can see a crack of daylight ahead; it is not far now.

I lurch into the open air and stumble, drunk and foolish

with freedom. The next moment I am falling, rolling, bone over bruised bone, not far but enough to be left winded, dazed, crucified with pain. Above me I can still hear the winsome music and twist my head a fraction to see the piper. The movement is agony. Beside the piper is a boy, wiry and slender, no older than I.

"Is he dead?" asks the boy.

"I don't think so," says the piper, "but the music didn't hold him. Perhaps he is deaf as well as crippled."

"Crippled?" says the boy.

"Oh yes, he could barely keep up with the others. So not much use even if he could hear my pipe."

"What if he tells his people?"

The piper laughs, a cold, hard laugh. "Unlikely. He can hardly move. A night on these hills should finish him. And if it doesn't, how will he find his way home? Or back here again? And who would believe him anyway? They will say that he left them sane and came back crazy. Poor boy. His ordeal unhinged him. Some may pity him but none will trust his story. Come – there is nothing to be gained here and much that we must do within."

Then the piper leads the way back into the tunnel but the boy hesitates. For one brief moment, his troubled eyes meet mine. Then he flicks back his dark hair, turns and is gone.

Tanith woke flailing, suffocated by the darkness and her terror. She had to get out but her hands met only cold stone. The waking was worse than the dream. She was screaming, her knuckles were raw with battering the walls and her legs paralyzed, dead from Wulfie's weight on them.

"Tanith! It's all right!"

Wulfie, howling, backed out of the hole and Crow half-dragged, half-shoved Tanith into the icy air where she lay, open-mouthed, taking great gulps, staring up at the white morning sky.

Crow reached out a hand, as if he was going to stroke her hair but Tanith grabbed it and held it so hard that he winced. Blood oozed from her grazed knuckles and dripped onto the snow.

"Show me," she said. "Show me what you've done with the kids!"

Crow wanted to explain, wanted to find food and water first, but Tanith wouldn't let him. They shared Crow's few remaining dried apples and crammed their mouths with fresh snow and then, reluctantly, Crow led the way further along the rock face.

"Why are we going this way?" asked Tanith, after a short distance. "You couldn't have got the kids this far while I was fighting off those hunters."

"There is more than one way in," said Crow. "We're going to a ventilation shaft. It's the way I got out years ago. It should be okay still."

"Got out?"

"Yes. The place I've taken the kids to. It was my home.

But I left. That's why I live in the city. Partly."

"Did you have to leave?"

"I wasn't forced to, if that's what you mean. I chose to go. I never wanted to come back."

"Why?"

Crow's face was grim. "You'll see," he said.

"What's the other part?"

"I'm sorry?"

"You said that was why you live in the city. Partly. But you didn't have to come to the city just because you didn't like it at home. So why did you?"

Crow glanced around warily. "If you must know, I was looking for my father. I wanted to find him. He left because he couldn't stand the place any longer either."

"But the kids? I thought you were taking them to somewhere safe."

"Oh, it's safe, all right," said Crow, bitterly.

"How do you mean? What's wrong with it?"

"I'm showing you, aren't I? That's what you wanted. Come on then. Let's get a move on. We're nearly there."

They rounded a craggy boulder which loomed out of the hillside like a stooped old crone and Crow pointed to a small opening at ground level, barely distinguishable from a large rabbit burrow.

"Down there?" said Tanith. Suddenly, she was flummoxed. This was granite country; you needed to travel beyond her home territory into the land of the white limestone to find potholes and caverns.

"I don't get it," she said, her mind dredging up the details of her grandmother's story. "There can't be caves under here – it's not the right rock."

"No, and I can't make children follow me by playing a pipe either, can I?" said Crow. "I can't make kids who were so tired they could barely walk in a straight line, run and leap and hurry after me as if they had all the energy in the world. But that's what you saw happen. Isn't it? And the hunters saw them too."

Slowly, Tanith nodded.

"So are we going down this hole or not?"

"If we go down, can we get out again?" said Tanith.

Crow looked her straight in the eye. "I can't guarantee that," he said. "I'm not popular down there. Of course it's possible to get out – I've done it before, haven't I? But I can't promise it'll be easy."

"I see," said Tanith. She had Wulfie's head in her hands and was fondling his ears nervously. "And you're sure the kids are safe?"

"Yes," said Crow. "The kids are safe. You think I'd send Timbo somewhere dangerous after the trouble I went to rescuing him? Or Asta? Or Jed? They're my friends!"

"If I didn't go with you," said Tanith, carefully, "if I wasn't forcing you, would you still go down there? Go back home?"

Crow stared into the distance.

"I don't want to," he said. "It would be far easier not to. Like I said, I'm not popular down there. And I still want to find my father. But when I came to find you, I promised Asta

I'd go back... All I did was take them to the gate and leave them with the doorkeeper. They won't know what's hit them. I ought to go and check on them. I ought to explain. I just don't want my... I don't want anyone to know I'm in there."

Tanith buried her fingers in Wulfie's fur, twisting it round and round.

"But you don't have to go? You could leave Asta and Jed and the kids and start all over again out here? They would be safe?"

"Yes," said Crow. "I could. In theory. We could both walk away. We don't have to follow them."

"And that would be safer for you?"

Crow nodded. He placed a hand on her shoulder, drawing her fractionally closer to him. Tanith ached to lift her face and let the kiss that was hovering happen. But she knew it would be like sipping from a poisoned chalice for them both.

She let out a sound which was half-laugh, half-sob.

"But then we would never forgive ourselves," she said. "You because you promised you'd go back and I because I'd let down my grandmother. And in the end, we would hate each other."

Crow let his hand drop. "Let down your grandmother?" he said. "Why?"

Tanith sighed. "It's complicated. A long story. But it's been leading me here. And if I'm ever going to find out the truth, I need to go down that hole."

Crow raised an eyebrow. "Will you tell me later?" he said. "We shouldn't be hanging around here."

"As soon as I can," said Tanith. "I promise."

"Then it's after you down the hole," said Crow.

"What about Wulfie?"

"He comes too."

22

There was more to the disorientating rush of Tanith's journey down the hole than a simple fall. She had sat, teetering on the brink, unable to launch herself for several minutes before Crow pushed her hard. Then there was a nauseating jolt to her head, an uncomfortable spinning sensation and she landed on a rough floor.

"Move," shouted Crow from above. "Wulfie's coming."

She barely had time to shuffle out of the way before the light was blocked by Wulfie's bulk. He landed, whimpered, belched and shook his big head. *So he feels as sick as I do,*

Tanith thought. She hauled him aside and the next minute, Crow landed beside them, clutching his stomach.

"Yuk, that was rough," he said. "But it's off-limits – not meant to be used. It's only a ventilation shaft after all. I suppose we get what we deserve."

"What happened then? Why do we feel so sick?"

"Some sort of mind-shield," said Crow. "It's designed to stop people falling in. You're not meant to push your way through. Anyway, come on. We need to get going."

They appeared to have landed in a rough pit. Tanith had no way of gauging the size because, within a few metres, it was pitch-dark. Crow, however, had been there before. He disappeared into the darkness but quickly returned holding a clay jar and sniffing at the contents.

"Hmm…" he said. "Should be enough." Then he thrust one end of his firestaff inside, pulled it out soaked, and lit it. Above her head, Tanith could now see that there were three holes in the pit roof, two of them obscured by vegetation. From the floor, two low tunnels led off in opposite directions.

"The one on the right," said Crow. "I'll go first. We'll have to crawl. Will Wulfie manage?"

They both looked at Wulfie dubiously. He had huge hip bones which splayed out like frog's legs when he crouched.

"I don't know," said Tanith. "But I guess we're just going to have to go for it. How far is it along the tunnel?"

"Maybe a hundred metres? I'm afraid we'll have to do it

in the dark. I can't carry a burning staff and crawl. It shouldn't be too bad. It's slightly downhill. It was worse coming up. I remember I kept slipping back."

Tanith gulped. She hated small spaces. Just being stuck in this underground pit was setting her pulse racing.

Crow seemed to sense her fear.

"Don't worry. I'll go first. It'll be fine. They have to keep it clear – that's why they have this maintenance pit.

"Wulfie had better be next so I know he's not got left behind," said Tanith.

"Fine," said Crow. "Let's go."

He stamped out his torch, swung his staff back into its place across his back, and crawled into the tunnel.

But Wulfie wouldn't follow him. Once Crow's feet had disappeared, the big dog sat back on his haunches and howled. Tanith hauled him up and tried to force him but he planted his feet firmly on the sandy floor and would not budge. Then he raised a paw, batted Tanith with it and whimpered.

"Crow!" Tanith yelled down the hole. "Wait! Wulfie won't come."

For a moment, Tanith thought he hadn't heard and was swamped by a nightmare vision of starving to death alone but for Wulfie. Then Crow's feet emerged and he was back.

"What shall we do?" asked Tanith. "I'm not leaving Wulfie here."

"You'll have to go first," said Crow. "He's bound to follow you. Then I'll bring up the rear. Don't worry – you can't get lost. Just be careful at the end – it drops down really steeply – more of a slide than a tunnel."

Tanith felt sick. The thought of going down that hole, without Crow's comforting presence ahead of her, panicked her instantly. She hadn't even begun and already her heart was pounding and her hands and face were clammy. But she wouldn't tell Crow.

"Right," said Tanith. "Okay. Better get on with it then."

"We'll be right behind you," said Crow. "Don't worry. Just keep going."

Tanith crouched down awkwardly. What lay ahead would have been challenging for an able-bodied person; for her it was excruciating. For a moment she considered telling Crow that she and Wulfie would wait for him in the pit while he checked on the others but supposing he never came back? She didn't want to end her days, chilled and thirsty in this icy tomb, knowing she had failed in her mission.

A hundred metres. She reckoned that each move of her stunted arms might be twenty-five centimetres. She could count her moves. Four hundred and she should be out the other side.

Her eyes had grown accustomed to the gloom of the pit but inside the tunnel the darkness was total. Even if it opened out, she would have no idea. Horror gripped her. Supposing she was actually crawling across a massive cave? She could travel in circles and never realize. She stopped and spread her arms around her; on every side she met rough, confining rock. She heaved a sigh of relief. She never would have thought she might be grateful to find herself cramped up in a tunnel. Wulfie's breath was warm against her legs and he nosed her buttocks impatiently. So he had followed. Thank goodness! The knowledge forced her onwards; he wouldn't be enjoying this any more than she was.

"Twenty-eight, twenty-nine, thirty," she breathed. The counting calmed her, helped to steady her mind. Every number spoken was one less to go. Every move of her arms was one fewer to make. Slowly, painfully, she inched her way along.

"Two hundred and ninety-nine, three hundred." Only another hundred to go. She was nearly there.

It was then that cramp struck. She could feel it in her toes first, twisting and locking. She tried to wriggle them, flexing them and her foot as much as she could, but it was no use. The hard, tight agony shot up her leg. She needed to hug her leg, rub it, swing it – anything and everything to get it out of its fixed position – but how could she? Almost weeping with pain and desperation, she hauled herself along, digging in her elbows to give herself more purchase, dragging her traitor leg behind.

"Four hundred and four, four hundred and five…" She should be there by now but there was no sign of any end to the suffocating darkness. Her panic was mounting again and she had just reached the point where she felt she couldn't restrain a scream any longer when suddenly, the light changed. It was fractionally less dark. No, she wasn't imagining it and yes, beneath her the floor was beginning to slope downwards, becoming skittery and slippery with gravel. She was starting to lose her grip, the rock beneath her fingers was damp and then she was sliding, losing all control of her body, finally falling face first onto a dirt path. She pulled herself aside just in time to avoid being crushed by Wulfie as he slithered out of the tunnel. Then she struggled into a sitting position so that she could get to work on her cramped leg.

Wulfie, however, stuck his nose back up the tunnel and whined.

"Crow?" said Tanith. She hobbled to the opening they had just shot out of and peered inside. "Crow? *Crow?*"

She could see only a little way. There was no sign of Crow. To her astonishment, the path she was standing on ran alongside an underground river – or was it a canal? The tunnel had remarkably smooth white sides, lit up gloomily by intermittent torches in wall sconces. Tanith considered her situation. This tunnel looked well used; Crow appeared to be stuck in the ventilation shaft. She was accompanied on an extremely narrow towpath by a very conspicuous dog. If someone came along now, it would be all too evident that she was an intruder. Crow had insisted that the kids were safe but both he and his father had left this place because they couldn't bear it. So how would an intruder be treated? Tanith had no idea.

"Crow!" she called again up the shaft. "Crow? Are you stuck?"

From what seemed a horribly long way up, she heard him. What was he saying? Something about his staff?

Tanith considered. Could she possibly climb back up that gravelly slide to help Crow? The thought of returning to the coffin-like darkness filled her with dread but what other options did she have? She was marooned in alien territory with no idea where she was going and anyway, she could hardly leave Crow stuck up the ventilation shaft to starve to death.

"Wulfie, stay!" said Tanith. He looked at her mournfully and whimpered again but when she reached into the shaft, he lay down and settled his head between his front paws. He understood, she was sure. And he would wait. She just had to pray that no one came along and found him.

If Tanith had thought coming down the shaft was hard, then going back up was almost impossible. Her cramped leg was still stiff and several times she slid back down the exit chute, despite digging her toes and elbows into the shifting gravel. After the fourth failed attempt, she took off her boots and socks. Feeling as if she was screwing the sides of her feet into the damp ground, she managed to get enough purchase to claw her way up. Once she was past the slide, it was easier. She was now so used to continual pain that she could almost ignore it. It made no difference to her progress at any rate.

"Crow!" she called, her voice hoarse with effort. "I'm coming!"

And to her intense relief, his reply sounded close.

Maybe if she just counted to thirty...

Suddenly, there he was. Her straining fingers touched his hair.

"I'm so sorry," he breathed, reaching out a hand and finding her cheek. "My firestaff's got caught on the roof somehow and I can't twist round enough to move it."

It took a few minutes for Tanith to free Crow and then they started the appalling journey back. But something in Tanith's heart was soaring. She could feel Crow's warm breath in her face, the occasional brush of his hair. She had rescued him. He had saved her life twice but now she had saved his. Whatever had happened to the kids, whatever lay ahead, whatever secrets Crow had kept from her, the bond between them had tightened and that both excited and frightened her.

23

They heard Wulfie barking just as Tanith felt the ground dipping away below her for the final slide.

"Oh no," Tanith gasped. "Someone's bound to hear him. Will he give us away? Are there any other dogs down here?"

"No," Crow grunted. "Dogs won't do what the pipers want. Can you call to him?"

But at that moment, Tanith hit the slide and shot away from Crow. Wulfie was almost delirious in his relief at seeing her. When she shouted at him to be quiet, he seemed to shrink, head drooping, tail between his legs, big eyes betrayed.

"Oh Wulfie, I'm sorry," Tanith said, hugging him. "But we need you to be really quiet. We don't want anyone to know we're here."

Crow, who had slid out of the shaft behind her, was standing very still, peering down the gloomy tunnel.

"Hush," he said, "I'm trying to listen."

Hurrying to pull on her socks and boots, Tanith strained to hear too. Wulfie was suddenly alert, ears back, nose up. In the distance, they could hear the splish of paddles and the murmur of urgent voices.

"Is there somewhere we can hide?" demanded Tanith.

"Ssh," said Crow. "We shouldn't need to."

He was feeling at his waist for his pouch. Fascinated, Tanith watched as he took out his tiny pipe and began to play.

The tune which filled the tunnel was nothing like the intoxicating music Tanith had heard on the hillside. Instead it was harsh and repellent, tuneful but in a driving, insistent way that made her head hurt. She put her fingers in her ears and grimaced at Crow.

"That's awful," she mouthed.

He winked at her but continued to play. Then he stopped, listened and nodded in satisfaction.

"Gone," he said. "We'll be all right for a bit now."

"Did you drive them away?" said Tanith in amazement. "Your own people?"

Crow shook his head. "I drove them away," he said, "but they weren't my own people. Working in this tunnel, they'd be outsiders."

"Outsiders?"

"People from outside – up there. Your world."

"This is a different world?"

"No, not really. It connects with yours, you've seen that. But we do things differently here. Come on – you said I was to show you, so let's go."

Crow set off at a brisk pace along the towpath with Tanith limping behind him. Without the rush of adrenalin which had driven her down and then back up the shaft, she felt so bruised, battered and exhausted that even a slow hobble seemed too much. She was light-headed and snappish with hunger and suddenly violently irritated with Crow. The agony of moving, of trying to be quick, was pushing her beyond the limits of her fierce self-control. Infuriating as it would have been if Crow made concessions for her, now she felt that he could, at least, slow down. And he hadn't even thanked her for that killing crawl back up to rescue him! She remembered the touch of his lips on her face and brushed at it irritably. Kiss him? Right now, she wondered what had possessed her to want to.

"Crow!" she shouted.

He turned. "Ssh!" he hissed, impatiently.

"Don't shush me!" Tanith snapped. "I can't keep up with you. Can't we rest for a little while somewhere?"

"There is nowhere," said Crow, as waspish as she was.

"And I thought you wanted me to show you the kids?"

"I do – of course I do! It's just…" Tanith turned her head aside, determined that he wasn't going to see the weakness that she was blinking away. "It's just that I simply can't carry on much longer."

"All right then," said Crow, tense and grumpy. "I've got an idea. Not far now, okay?"

Crow was cross with himself and cross with Tanith. It had been stupid to get his firestaff stuck like that. He'd frightened himself badly and made himself look an idiot. Worse, it meant it was his fault that Tanith was in so much pain now. Crawling back up the shaft must have really hurt. Part of him wanted to believe that it served her right. She hadn't let him explain about the kids but had insisted that they set off immediately to find them. He had wanted to wait and talk things through, tell her the full story. There would have been time to hunt down something to eat and cook it over a fire in their little bolt-hole. He could have boiled up some snow with some of the precious dried willow bark he carried and given it to her to drink; that would have eased the pain in her joints somewhat. Instead, they had blundered on and now she was hurting worse than ever. Well, silly girl. She shouldn't have been so impatient.

But in his heart, he knew she had right on her side. He had never been open with her, never been fully honest. If she, waking in the dark, terrified by whatever nightmare had gripped her, demanded to see that the kids were safe, who was he to demand a chance to explain? He was the one who had spirited them away. There had been numerous chances to tell her the truth and he had never taken them, afraid that she would leave. And as each day passed and he became convinced that she was unique – an outsider over whose mind he had no control – he knew that he could not bear to lose her. So he had done what she wanted and now what a mess they were in, tired, starving and angry, the bond between them a pain as much as a pleasure.

He forced himself to slow his furious pace. He turned, stopped, waited. The sight of Tanith struggling along, holding her dog for support, was pitiful. But her chin was up, her expression stony. He sighed. It must have been torture for her to swallow her pride and confess that she couldn't keep up. She wouldn't thank him for it but he couldn't let her battle on without at least asking.

"Tanith," he said. "Please... I'm not as tough as you. Don't make me watch you suffer. I could carry you."

The fight within played out on her mobile face. At last, reluctantly, she spoke.

"All right," she said. "But not for long."

Crow stooped slightly and swung her up. She wrapped her arms round his neck and let her head slump against his shoulder. As she relaxed against him, he could feel the tension in his own body melt, loosening his stride. Even Wulfie seemed to be smiling.

"Not far now, I promise," Crow said.

He could hear the limp smile in her voice. "To tell you the truth," she said, "I'm past caring."

Crow walked quickly, despite his burden. Before long they could hear voices and the random creaks and splashes of boats in use.

"What is it?" whispered Tanith.

"It's a loading bay," said Crow. "I'd better put you down while I scout around a bit."

Ahead of them, Tanith could see that the canal opened out beyond a rough-hewn arch into a well-lit wharf area. A number of flat-bottomed punts were drawn up, some empty, some piled high with large roll-shaped packages. Crow pushed her and Wulfie into a recess behind the archway.

"Stay here," he said. "I shouldn't be long."

Crow pulled out his little pipe pouch from inside his belt and let it hang where it could be seen. Then he strode out confidently from behind the arch and tapped a young man on the shoulder. The man jumped, nearly dropping the large roll that he was hefting onto a punt.

"Sorry," said Crow. "Didn't mean to startle you. Quality check. One medium, please. Quick as you can."

"But sir," said the young man. "These have all been checked and wrapped already."

Crow looked him firmly in the eye. "Random check," he said. "There's been a complaint. She's not at all happy."

The young man didn't argue. He found a hooked pole

and dragged in an empty punt. Then he stripped the wrapping off a medium-sized roll and heaved it inside.

Tanith, peering cautiously round the arch, watched, fascinated. Inside the roll was a rug. What was Crow up to?

She soon found out.

"Have I to take it to her?" asked the young man.

"No, I'll do that," said Crow. "You'd better get back to work. Sorry to have interrupted."

Then he picked up one of the huge poles from a rack on the wharf and stepped into the loaded punt. He pushed off and, with a few deft shoves, sent it skimming under the arch towards Wulfie and Tanith.

"Now," he whispered. "All we have to do is roll you and Wulfie up inside this rug."

"What?" said Tanith.

"You heard," said Crow. "It'll be a good chance for you to have a rest."

"But…" Tanith stopped. It was a good idea. Wherever they had to get to, she didn't have the strength to carry on.

Crow unrolled the rug carefully. Tanith gasped. Even in the dim light of the tunnel, she could see that it was beautiful, an intricate maze of interlocking shapes. She reached out her hand. It was so soft that suddenly she couldn't wait to lie down and let Crow enshroud her in its luxurious folds.

"Is it wool?" she asked.

Crow nodded. "Yes – spun extremely fine," he said.

The rug was wide and overlapped the sides of the punt.

Gingerly, Tanith lay on it, the top of her head lined up with the edge. "Wulfie!" she called, and there was a terrifying lurch as he leaped aboard. Then he quietly settled down alongside her and Crow flipped the rug over them. Tanith had a moment of panic as the wool closed over her face but she tilted her chin so that she could still breathe and then found herself relaxing into its cosy pile. Startled, Wulfie whined, then licked Tanith's face, making her giggle.

"It's all very well for you to laugh," hissed Crow. "I'm going to have to do all the hard work!"

Tanith felt the shudder as Crow pulled the pole up and then they were off, gliding smoothly through the water, the motion and the softness of the woolly tufts massaging her quickly into a warm, deep sleep.

24

Music! I love music! I drag myself into the street, desperate to find its source. We have had no music for so long, no joyful melodies or merry tunes, only miserable complaining and whining and moaning and always, always, there in the background, the scritching and scratching and squealing of rats.

And here he is, the musician himself, a tall, dark, rangy figure, sweeping along our main street, his coloured robes softening his angular frame, his high, wide-brimmed hat shading his fine, pale face. The pipe he plays is tiny but the sound seems to fill the valley and billow out beyond.

I am intoxicated, drunk with joy. I feel as if my spirit has been as crippled as my body and now it is untwisting, loosening, stretching, preparing for flight. I cannot run after the piper but I would if I could. I would hang onto his robes and beg him to teach me to play like that too.

Around me, the street is filling up fast. The whole town seems to be flocking out to see this wonder. Music lovers or not, they all want a piece of the excitement.

At the end of the street, stands the town hall. The piper stops before it and takes the pipe from his mouth. The people fall back into a circle around him, an orderly mass. There is no pushing or shoving, arguing or kicking. A strange silence falls as the piper's gaze rakes the crowd.

"For a thousand gold coins," he cries. "I will rid your town of rats!"

No one speaks. I stare up into their frozen faces. There is something odd here, something uncanny. It is as if they are entranced.

"A thousand gold coins!" says the mayor, in a distant voice. "We would pay fifty thousand!"

Fifty thousand gold coins? It is more than the town is worth! But no one argues. No one says a word. Have they all lost their senses but for me?

"Done," says the piper and again lifts his pipe to his lips.

"No," I scream. "Don't do it! Don't trust him! He's bewitched you!"

But no one hears me and the piper simply raises an eyebrow and starts to play.

And so the horror begins.

Tanith woke with a start, but the rug imprisoned her and stifled her scream. Even so, Crow, alert to every sound, heard it.

"It's all right, Tanith," he said. "It must have been a dream. You're in the rug, remember? And we're nearly there. Just hang on!"

Tanith struggled to speak. "But I have to talk to you... I have to ask you something... I need to know..." she gasped.

But Crow was busy manoeuvring the punt into the bank. Moments later, he unrolled her from her warm prison. She struggled to her feet and grabbed his arms.

"Crow, I—"

"Sssh! I can hear something. On the water. Listen!"

Sure enough, from round the bend in the canal, they could hear the watery glide of a punt approaching.

"Your pipe?" whispered Tanith.

"No – up here! Quick!"

They had stopped beside an archway shielding a spiral staircase carved into the rock. Crow pushed Tanith inside and she started climbing, dragging Wulfie by the collar. Above her, she could hear a deadened thumping but she couldn't place it and didn't stop to ask. She could sense

Crow's urgency behind her and summoned up energy she didn't know she had.

At the top of the stairwell hung a heavy drape – a fine, wool rug. Crow pushed past Tanith and peered round it carefully.

"Once we're through here, turn right and up the stairs again," he whispered. "As fast as you can."

Tanith's heart sank, but she did as she was told, darting into the second stairwell without a backward glance. Then she scrambled after Crow, her heart thudding, until thankfully, she emerged on a rock gallery, barred off from the room below by a simple rail. Wulfie bounded after her but sat at her murmured command. Below her she could now hear the thumping clearly but it was softened by mesmeric, haunting pipe music which fitted its beat exactly. She didn't dare peep down.

Crow pulled her to the back, where the gallery was shadowed by overhanging rock.

"Now crawl forwards and look!" he hissed in her ear. "If the kids aren't here already, they soon will be!"

Curiously, Tanith did as she was told, keeping as low as she could and peering between the solid wooden struts which supported the rail. Below her lay a scene of medieval industry.

Row upon row of upright looms filled the massive cavern that lay beneath the gallery. It was lit by huge torches in wall sconces and suspended in robust candelabras from the ceiling. Even so the light was dim, giving Tanith the confidence to peer out more boldly. At each loom, perched on a smooth wooden bench, sat one or perhaps two children, their fingers busy with tufting and weaving. They worked steadily in time with the music. No adult supervised them but the children didn't chat or break from their work. Tanith searched for the piper; there had to be one somewhere. Then, at last, following her ears, she looked up and, sure enough, on the far side of the cavern was a gallery mirroring theirs. Resting on the rail and playing, was a young woman.

Tanith shuffled back, appalled.

"How old are those kids?" she hissed. "Some of them are tiny!"

"The youngest are six or seven," said Crow. "The oldest maybe fourteen, fifteen? It depends how big they grow. Fingers need to be tiny and nimble for this work. However skilled they are, eventually their fingers get too big. And sometimes…" Crow stopped and she could hear him swallow a couple of times. "Sometimes they have to stop because they can't see properly any more. The lighting – the fine work – it isn't good…"

He stopped, gagged by the look of horror on Tanith's face.

"And you…you've brought our kids here? I don't believe it!" Her voice was incautiously loud.

"*Our* kids?" Crow was strained almost to breaking point and careless too, insulted by her tone. "What d'you mean? Since when have they been *your* kids? Who's been looking after them for years? Not you! What right have you to criticize?"

"Ssh!" said Tanith, urgently. "Someone will hear you!"

But it was too late. The haunting music had stopped. Whether the piper on the far gallery had heard them or caught a glimpse of their movement didn't matter. She had spotted them now and her reaction was immediate.

"Intruders!" she yelled into the yawning space below her and then, from her tiny pipe came an ear-piercing shriek of baffling volume.

Immediately, the children stopped weaving and broke into an excited babble, gazing around curiously, pointing and staring and giggling like ordinary kids.

"Quick!" said Crow. "Through here!"

At the back of the gallery another rug draped a doorway and Crow bundled Tanith and Wulfie through into a narrow tunnel.

It was hopeless. Already, they could hear running footsteps coming towards them. Crow turned back, his fingers flying to his belt for his pipe but as he and Tanith barged onto the gallery, a guard leaped out of the stairwell, closely followed by others.

They were trapped, guards both ahead and behind. Wulfie leaped, felling the first guard but a fierce blow to his head from the second knocked him out. It took seconds for them to overpower Tanith and not much longer for them to have Crow armlocked and bound, his firestaff tossed into the cavern beneath them.

"I'm so sorry," Crow mouthed at Tanith but she just shook her head, bewildered. The jigsaw pieces of nightmare which had been amassing in her head were slotting into her grandmother's story. Faced with the horror that Crow had brought her to, capture seemed trivial. He had betrayed the kids and had almost fooled her too. She twisted her head back desperately, imagining the guards hurling Wulfie's body over the rail. They didn't but two hoicked him up roughly between them. She couldn't see if he was breathing or not and felt as if her heart was being wrenched from her chest. Her whole being was in agony. For the first time in her life, the pain felt almost too great to bear.

25

The guards shoved Tanith and Crow down the spiral stairs, through the carpet cavern and out through another draped doorway. Wincing with every step, Tanith still had the wit to notice that order had been restored among the children, each again sitting calmly at his or her loom, the hypnotic melody once more keeping them spellbound. Their faces were peaceful and content but something rebelled in Tanith. It was contrary, she knew, but she would do anything to keep control of her own mind and her freedom, however painful, rather than exchange it for that controlled tranquillity. And then, despite the guard's rough hand at her neck and the agony in her heart, she had a moment of real insight. For some time now she had understood that whatever mind powers Crow had, they had no significant effect on her. Perhaps it was her lifelong experience of suffering that made her immune? To know that she could live with pain and survive to be joyful was perhaps a powerful protection against Crow's seductive powers. Maybe her mind was suspicious of the promise of bliss and so couldn't be captured? That thought gave her courage and strength. Whatever lay ahead, she had endured a long apprenticeship in rising above torture. Wulfie might be dead, Crow might prove to have betrayed her and all the other kids might be enslaved, but she was not going to go under.

They arrived at another draped doorway. As a guard pulled aside the carpet, Tanith saw that it was thick and heavy and richly woven with gold. Whoever was inside was important.

She and Crow were unceremoniously thrust through the arch into a cave that made Tanith gasp in wonder. The rough walls were gilded, every entrance was curtained with a sumptuous carpet woven in reds and golds, torches flared from intricately wrought black sconces and the floor was covered in a circular rug, the pile of which was so deep that Tanith's feet sank into it as if it were sand.

A guard prodded Tanith in the back. "Forward," he said.

Tanith obeyed but Crow held back. The guard cuffed him.

"I said, forward!" he bellowed.

Tanith flinched. Whatever he had done, she hated to see Crow struck. She craned round, trying to find Wulfie. Two guards were about to dump him on the ground.

"Gently!" she said, in a voice which surprised her, it held such authority. Startled, the guards obeyed.

A laugh rang out from the far end of the room and Tanith turned to see a tall, blonde-haired woman clapping as if vastly entertained.

"Bravo!" she said, coming towards them, the combination of her flowing multi-coloured robes and the deadening depth of the carpet giving the impression that she was gliding. Unnerved, Tanith wanted to step back but the guard was right behind her.

"So," said the woman, "who is this that my scapegrace son has brought home with him at last?"

Tanith's chin shot up and her mouth dropped open, her eyes meeting the woman's in a moment of stabbing shock.

The woman laughed again. "Oh, he didn't tell you then? No, I don't expect he did. He's left us once. Didn't want anything to do with us. Doubtless he hasn't told you the truth about his origins."

Crow, held by a guard on each side, twisted his head so that he could look at Tanith. His eyes were pleading. She knew he was begging her to understand. And she wanted to. She really wanted to understand why Crow had brought her and the kids to this place.

"He wanted to explain," she said. "But he hasn't had the opportunity."

The woman raised an eyebrow. "Really? You surprise me. I had always thought my son was an opportunist of the first order. But perhaps he has changed since he left us."

Crow's head was up now, his pale face quivering with anger.

"Stop toying with us, Mother," he said. "Don't you want to know what I'm doing here?"

His mother laughed again but there was no warmth there, only barely suppressed rage.

"I had thought it was obvious," she said. "A raggle-taggle bunch of city kids are thrust in at our door with the message that Crow has sent them. They are footsore, undernourished, lousy and filthy. We know enough about what it's like in the cities, Crow. We have our information. I tried to warn you. Life is tough and getting worse. You want back in. Well, my son, you'll have to do a bit better than that, I'm afraid. Two or three dozen scum of the earth isn't much of a peace offering after an absence of – what is it? – nearly five years? Five years when I had use for a gifted piper."

Crow's lip curled. "You are wrong, Mother," he said. "So wrong. As always. You never did understand me – or my father. That's one reason he left too."

Crow's mother stepped forward, lifted her arm and slapped him so hard across the cheek that even the guards started.

"You know *nothing* about why your father left," she snapped. "Take his pipe." Crow arched and struggled but there was nothing he could do. In an instant, a guard had slit the thong that held the pipe pouch and handed it to Crow's mother. She slid it out, looked at it disdainfully and then snapped it in two.

Unbidden, tears bled from Tanith's eyes. The woman's ruthlessness stabbed her in the guts. She ached to talk to Crow. This was no betrayal. She didn't understand his behaviour yet but she was sure his mother was wrong. Everything she had learned about him cried out against the idea that Crow was using the kids to buy his way back in.

"Confine the boy until I've decided what to do with him," said Crow's mother.

"What about the kids?"

"Oh, clean them, feed them, let them rest and set them to work tomorrow. We might as well use what he's brought."

"And the girl and the dog?"

"Put them in with my son. Let him try to explain himself, now that she knows the truth, now that she knows how much he has chosen to hide. How far, I wonder, do his powers extend?"

Tanith almost smiled. The woman didn't know everything about Crow. And she knew nothing about her.

As soon as they'd been thrust into a small, rough cave and the curtain drawn behind them, Crow began to apologize.

"I'm so sorry…" he started. "You must have thought… I never explained… You…"

"Ssh!" said Tanith. "Later. I have to see to Wulfie now."

She kneeled down beside the big dog and stroked his rough flank.

"He's warm," she said, "and I can feel his heartbeat." Even so, tears swamped her eyes and she had to brush them aside impatiently. It was terrible to see her old friend hurt like this.

"Wulfie," she croaked, close to his ear. "Wulfie, it's me, Tanith." Gently, she cupped her hand beneath his nose. One eye opened. Feebly, he lifted his head, his tongue reaching for her fingers.

"Concussion," said Crow. "He just needs to rest. There's nothing else we can do."

"You don't think they fractured his skull?" said Tanith.

Crow shook his head. "No – he wouldn't move if they had. And he'd be far worse. Really – believe me – I've been concussed a couple of times myself. He'll get over it."

"How long?" Tanith's voice was fretful.

"Don't know really. Maybe a couple of days? Anyway, we're not going anywhere at the moment. You need to rest, we all need some food – I'm sure she'll send some – and there's a powerful mind-lock on that doorway that I'm not sure I can overcome."

Tanith nodded. A mind-lock. That figured. "I think," she said, "I think it's time we talked."

26

A guard brought two steaming bowls of stew, chunky with root vegetables, a couple of hunks of bread and a pitcher of icy water, all of which Tanith and Crow fell on ravenously. A second guard threw in a bone for Wulfie but he merely sniffed it and went back to sleep.

"Mmm...mutton stew," said Crow. "Haven't eaten it for years. Almost makes me want to come home."

"Mutton?" said Tanith. "They keep sheep then?"

"Of course. Where do you think the wool comes from for the carpets? We stay hidden in these caves but some of our

outsiders live on the hills with the flocks. Wild places –
where your kind fear to go these days. I loved being sent
out there with my pipe when I was growing up. I suppose
that was one of the reasons I left – one of the more selfish
reasons."

"You wouldn't really want to come back would you?"
asked Tanith.

Crow snorted. "Are you mad? You've just met my
mother! I know she's sent us some decent food – I don't
suppose she'd let me starve to death – but there's no love
lost between us, as you've seen."

"Is she…is she the Queen or something?"

Crow nodded. "In effect, yes. She rules here. She's the
Pied Piper. If I'd stayed…" Here Crow gave a bitter little
shrug. "I'd be the heir. The next Pied Piper. But I couldn't do
that. You've seen what we do."

"I'm beginning to see," said Tanith, slowly. "The Pied
Piper. So that's who she is." She hesitated. "Do you
remember what I promised before we came down here?"

Crow nodded. "Of course. You were going to tell me
your story as soon as you could. About your grandmother."

"That's now then, isn't it?" said Tanith. "I've wanted to
tell you before but wasn't sure that I should."

"Because?"

"Because my story – my grandmother's story, that is –
and the strange dreams I've been having are about all this.
About what's happened. Well, sort of. They're about a man
with a pipe that played magical music. First he used it to

clear a town of rats. And then he used it to steal all the children. Asta knows a similar story. She says you won't let her tell it to the kids in case it frightens them. And that's because its true, isn't it, Crow? The man in the story was called the Pied Piper too."

Crow's face was bleak. "There are lots of stories like that," he said. "We have stolen outsiders' children on many occasions. Usually one here, one there – you'll have heard the warnings. Don't follow the marsh lights. Don't step inside the fairy ring. Sometimes we leave a piper child in the outsider's place – it's one way of getting intelligence."

Tanith's mouth dropped open. "But those are stories about *elves*!" she gasped. "Fairy stories. They're not *true*. Are they?"

Crow shrugged. "What do *you* think? Look around you. Is all this a figment of your imagination?"

"Are you saying that you're an *elf*? A *fairy*?"

Crow shrugged again. "Call us what you like. We call ourselves pipers. There are others like us in different parts of the world. We trade with them. We're all reliant on humans to do our work for us and we all find them in the same sorts of ways. Our gifts vary. But we're certainly not human."

"But why do you need humans to do your work? I never thought elves took slaves! I thought they were noble... wise...healers..."

Crow smiled wryly. "I know. We've been cunning over the years. We do have strange powers and we cover our tracks well. But the truth is, we do steal children. Occasionally dozens have been taken. Pipers do not breed easily. The birth of a child is rare. We are very few. To survive, we have to use others to work for us."

"I think you do more than survive," said Tanith. "It seems to me the pipers live in luxury."

Crow flushed. "Exactly," he said. "And that is why my father left – and then I followed. Our lifestyle is dependent on the exploitation of outsiders."

"The kids at the looms looked cared for," said Tanith. "Well-fed and clothed. I suppose that's something."

"Yes," said Crow. "They are not unhappy. Not nowadays. The guards who have imprisoned us here are outsiders too. You don't see them rebelling, do you? They are well-fed, clothed, entertained – they live together in communities, free in the evenings from the power of the pipe – for a few short hours. They grow up, fall in love, have children. Some work as farmers, some as shepherds, some as couriers. There is other work too. We mine rare minerals and make beautiful jewellery. We work with metal and hew out new caves. Those who have little skill in crafts but prefer to stay inside are miners, guards, cleaners, cooks. Few contract the sickness; they don't get chance to mix freely with the Citz or the Cratz. They live safe, happy lives – but always controlled by a piper and a pipe."

"So you were right," said Tanith. "This *is* a safe place to bring the kids."

Crow sank his head into his hands, running his fingers

distractedly through his hair. "Yes but they're not free – they will never be free again!"

Tanith said nothing. Now she understood. It all made sense. His moodiness, his irritability, his evident unhappiness on their journey. She quailed at the enormity of the decision he had had to make.

Crow was up and pacing the cave.

"I can't explain to you how I've agonized," he said. "All the time I've been helping the city kids I've known I could bring them here and they would be safe – but at what cost? I got out because I couldn't bear to be part of it any longer – how could I bring them here? All I could do was my best to help them in the city! But then I started to hear rumours – and how could I ignore them? What was better? To let these little kids be taken for *meat* or to bring them here? Safety and captivity? Or freedom and death? Which would you choose?"

He glared at Tanith, his eyes boring into her.

"Oh, I know, for yourself what you'd choose. The same as me – you'd rather run the risk of the sickness, bear all the hardships of the city, live each day dangerously, than give up your will. But for these little kids? What would you choose for them?"

Tanith hauled herself to her feet and laid her hand on his arm.

"There was no choice, Crow," she said. "You did the right thing."

He turned ferocious tear-bright eyes on her.

"You're not just saying that?" he demanded. "You really believe that's true?"

"Yes," said Tanith. "I would have done the same."

Crow dashed the tears away with the back of his hand. "I have to find Asta and Jed. They're stuck here too," he said. "I have to explain."

Tanith nodded. "Of course," she said. "But first you must explain more to me."

Crow slumped to the floor again and pulled his knees up to his chest.

"Yes," he said. "Yes, I must. You should know everything."

"So tell me then," said Tanith. "For you, there's more to your power than pipe magic – isn't there?"

Crow groaned. "Oh how I wish there wasn't," he said. "You have no idea how lonely it is."

"Then tell me," said Tanith. "You have no power over me."

Crow looked round the cave anxiously.

"Do you think we can be overheard?" he asked.

"I don't know. You know more about this place than I do. Let's just sit close together in the middle." She shuffled nearer so that she was beside his tense, hunched body, without touching. She was very wary. His mother had seemed so harsh; she had only put them in a cell together to torment them. If she found out how different things were, Tanith felt sure they would be separated.

"Okay," she said. "Tell me then."

Crow took a deep breath. "Occasionally," he said, "maybe once in a generation, a specially gifted piper is born. He or she has an additional power, not just the power of the pipe."

"A kind of mind power?" said Tanith.

"Yes, I suppose that's how you would describe it. It's a bit like what outsiders call hypnosis. We can make people do what we want just by looking into their eyes: wipe their memories, calm them down, make ourselves attractive to them – that sort of thing."

"You do it to Asta," Tanith interrupted. "You do it to the kids."

Crow nodded. "Yes – I tried not to, when I first came to the city. What was the point of leaving a place where we controlled the will of our captives with our music, only to control others with my mind? But it was the kids that made me do it. They were so helpless and there was so much I could teach them – help them to survive. But, of course, they wouldn't trust me. What child would these days? 'Here, little boy, I can help you if you let me.' They weren't stupid, even the most desperate ones. And I'm not naturally good with kids. Not like Asta. But I couldn't bear to see them struggle. I couldn't bear to see them dying for want of a few skills that I could teach them, for want of a bit of basic care."

"Yes," said Tanith. "It's puzzled me – the way they are drawn to you. Is that why you took up with Asta – because she's good with kids?"

Crow's eyes were fixed on the floor. "She was attracted to me. She made that very obvious. And she's clever and resourceful as well as great with kids."

"So you used her? So there was someone there for the kids all the time?"

"Yes. At first. I'm not proud of myself. But I've become very fond of her. That's why I have to tell her what this place is like – give her the chance to escape if she wants to. I owe it to her."

"Of course," said Tanith. "You must."

Crow let out a long, shuddering sigh.

"You don't know how much I hate myself," he said. "I'm so ashamed. I hate the way I haven't been able to avoid using my powers. I hate the way I've deceived Asta, the way I've controlled her mind. I hate the fact that I've brought the kids here... I tried so hard not to..."

"Hush," said Tanith. "It's not your fault. What could you do? You're a piper, not a human. Why not use your powers? You were trying to help, not hurt anyone! It's not as bad as what the piper did in my grandmother's story. It's not as bad as my dreams. I don't think the outsiders are always the innocent victims, you know. Think of the Cratz. Maybe they deserve to lose their freedom."

"Tell me," said Crow. "Tell me the story. We keep getting distracted."

Tanith screwed up her face. "My grandmother's story is quite short," she said. "But there are gaps. The strange thing is that my dreams are telling me the same story – and filling the gaps. D'you think that's possible? Or does that sound completely mad?"

"You haven't said I'm mad, have you?" said Crow. "Even though I've said I can control people's thoughts? Even though I've admitted I'm what you call an elf? So tell me the story."

"There was a town," said Tanith. "Or a village. I'm not really sure. Anyway, it was suffering from a plague of rats. It was so bad that the people were starving. They kept thinking it would pass, that of all their attempts to get rid of the rats, something had to work. But nothing did. Babies starved to death, toddlers died from festering rat wounds, old people were killed by strange illnesses. Then, one day, a man arrived. He called himself the Pied Piper. He wore odd, multi-coloured robes and carried a pipe. He promised that he would get rid of the rats for a huge fee. The villagers agreed. They had nothing to pay with but they were desperate. And, sure enough, the piper led all the rats down to the river and they drowned. Or that's the story, anyway. I always thought rats could swim."

"A skilled piper would pipe them to death," said Crow. "The music would tell them to sink and not come up."

"I see," said Tanith, with a shudder. "Anyway, the townspeople couldn't pay the bill. Perhaps that's what the Piper intended. He took up his pipe again and then all the children came tumbling out of the houses and followed him up into the mountains and that was the last anyone ever saw of them. The only reason anyone knows what happened is that one little boy was disabled – just like me. He tried to follow, not because the pipe was telling him to but because he was curious. He saw what happened – saw the children swallowed up into the mountain and somehow found his way back down, desperate to raise the alarm. But when he got back to the village, everyone was sleeping peacefully as if nothing was wrong. His parents had always been harsh and disappointed in him so at first he thought they were just glad to be rid of him – but when the town awoke next morning, he found that no one at all remembered him. He tried to speak about the missing children but no one would listen. They called him a mad boy and drove him away with stones. They said there had never been any children there and that he was a wicked, wicked liar. Even his own parents claimed they didn't recognize him and pelted him with dung from their midden. He couldn't understand it. In the end, he decided that they must all be pretending they couldn't remember the children – that they were anxious to be rid of all those hungry mouths. After all, no adult had followed the children to see where the Piper took them.

"The boy couldn't bear to stay any longer. He left the village to make his own way in the world but he always remembered the children and intended to go back to rescue them. He had seen inside the mountain and it had horrified him. When the boy was old and grey and still hadn't gone back, it haunted him. On his deathbed, he begged his son to search, but of course, he didn't. Why should he care about a bunch of children he never knew and a story that sounded like a fairy tale? But on *his* deathbed, he told the story too. And so it has passed on until my grandmother told it to me, just before she died. And I, because she begged me to, set out to discover what became of the children."

Crow's face was grim. "It's a story I know," he said. "My father told it to me. That piper was one of my ancestors. It's a shameful blot on our family, a hideous misuse of our mind power."

"Mind power?" said Tanith. "But wasn't he just an ordinary piper?"

Crow shook his head. "Think about it. The music doesn't make people forget things. It just makes them do what the piper wants. But the boy got back to the village and everyone had forgotten the children. How could that be? You really think that they would all gang up and pretend they'd forgotten their own children? That they were all monsters? That they wouldn't have tried to follow the piper when the children ran after him? He couldn't hold them off with his music and lead the children away at the same time. But they stayed in the village and didn't follow. That piper wiped their memories."

"And somehow I'm tapping into the boy's memories..." said Tanith. "Sharing his pain... It's coming back to me now. The mayor offered fifty thousand gold coins to the piper and the boy couldn't understand why no one argued. They all stayed quiet – as if they were in a trance."

"There you are then," said Crow, triumphantly. "I told you I knew this story. It was one of the biggest kidnaps of outsiders ever. But in our version, the villagers *refused* to pay the piper for getting rid of the rats – so he took the children. In your version, he bewitched them and tricked them. My father always said he must have been a mind worker to capture so many."

"And he was one of your ancestors?"

"Yes. Nothing to be proud of, is it? My father's family is one of the most important in the piper world, thanks to him. That's why my father ended up bound to my mother, even though they had nothing in common. It was an arranged marriage. My mother's family are immensely skilled pipers; my father's also have the mind power. The old Pied Piper, my grandfather, hoped that I would be wondrously powerful in both."

"And you are," said Tanith.

"Yes, but my father taught me to hide it well. He quickly learned how cold my mother is and so did I. Even as a toddler I ran to my father, not to her. So it was he who learned about my mind power and he who taught me to hide it from her, so she couldn't force me to use it for whatever selfish ends she had."

"What happened to your father?" Tanith asked.

"He left. He tried to stay until I was a fully trained piper but I think he was beginning to lose his mind; he couldn't bear to stay in a place he hated so much."

"And he didn't take you with him?" Tanith was shocked.

"There was a terrible row. For years we'd survived with outsiders who'd been born and bred in the caves. But my mother wanted to expand. She wanted to start lead mining again. My father didn't – he didn't like her reasons and he didn't like what it used to do to the outsiders."

"What were her reasons?"

"I don't know – greed probably. My father didn't tell me – he just said she was messing with human ideas that were better left alone. But I know what it did to the outsiders. It's dreadful heavy work and over time, it kills them."

"Of course," said Tanith. "I know. We mined lead too, for hundreds of years. It slowly poisoned the workers."

"Maybe that's what the boy in your dream saw inside the mountain," said Crow. "Little kids crushing lead ore. Little kids mining. Anyway, my father left. He thought I was too young to take then but he wanted me to follow him to the city when I was old enough. So as soon as I could, I did. And look where it's got me. Right back here where I started from."

Tanith gripped Crow's hand.

"I'm sorry," she said.

"It wasn't meant to be like this. I was supposed to find him once I got out. Maybe he didn't realize how big the city is. Maybe he's dead. Whatever. But I haven't found him yet. And perhaps now I never will."

"Don't be stupid," said Tanith. "You're just tired. We're getting out of here, don't you worry. Then you can find your father."

27

I am peering round a rough-hewn archway into a cavern so vast I can scarcely see its ceiling and the noise of the workers below is softened by the great height.

I can make little of what they are doing but that it is hard and heavy. It seems to be simply a process of hammering rock into smaller pieces and sorting it. It is unlike quarrying for the pieces are too small and I know of no precious mineral that could be mined in these parts. But what truly appals me is the workers.

They are children, little children, younger than me, waifs with stick-thin arms and legs, dressed in coarse woollen hose and jerkins, whether they are girls or boys; in fact, it is hard to tell. Their hair is close-cropped, maybe so as not to interfere with their hammering, maybe because of lice, and none is old enough for their sex to be obvious. They all work doggedly, ignoring the disturbance caused by the arrival of the piper and a few score new children. Their eyes are wide and blank, as if stretched to the limits of their vision, for the light is dim and there is an unhealthy bluish tinge to their pallor. As I watch, one child falls, dropping its hammer, its body slumped as if utterly exhausted but, trance-like, its little arm keeps on hammering the empty air.

Beyond the arch, the piper is talking to another man, in similar garb but richer, a polished pipe swinging from his belt.

"This is a most fine achievement," says the second man. "With these we can expand our production massively. And you are sure the parents will remember nothing?"

"Certain," says the piper.

"Excellent. You have served our people exceptionally well. Your name will go down in the history of our people. This is a turning point. No longer will we struggle to survive. It is the start of great and glorious things."

All this time, the children from my village stand silently together. Gone are the merry, laughing voices, the scampering and capering. They seem transfixed, unable to speak or move. I don't stop to think. I am simply desperate to break the spell.

"John!" I shout. "Marion! Hubert!" The names of the first children I can see spring to my lips. "John! Wake up! Marion – this way! You must escape!"

It is a stupid, mindless act but I am horrified and helpless. The children don't hear me, of course. They are safe in their tomb-like trance. But the pipers do and the second immediately raises his pipe to his mouth, thinking to hold me.

But his music has no power over me and at once I am down the passageway, stumbling back to freedom, guilt already heavy on my soul.

Tanith woke, sobbing quietly, curled up between Wulfie and Crow, stiff and uncomfortable but thankfully, warm.

Crow stirred in his sleep. "What is it?" he murmured. "Another dream?"

"Yes," she said. "It was so sad. It was worse then. You were right about the lead-mining, I think. The poor children – it's so much better now. And the boy. He felt so guilty for leaving them behind."

Crow propped himself up on one elbow and rubbed his eyes. "What?" he said. "You're not making sense."

Quickly, Tanith explained. "So you see," she said. "It could be worse. At least your mother feeds and clothes them properly. At least the work isn't so unpleasant and dangerous. At least they have *some* happiness."

Crow wasn't impressed. "What a people to belong to," he

said. "What a history. Cruelty and exploitation. Fantastic."

"It's no worse than what humans do," said Tanith. "And it's better now. You have to admit that."

Crow snorted. "Only because the alternative's being butchered! Sorry – my mistake. My mother's a saint really."

"Crow," said Tanith. "Stop it. It isn't your fault. You can't change the past. You can only do your bit to improve it now. And you have."

"Great. I feel so much better. Thanks, Tanith."

Tanith sighed. He was so hard to reach, so determined to be bitter and negative. Why wouldn't he understand that he wasn't to blame for any of this? And why couldn't he see the positive side? She supposed he didn't have the insight of her dreams. How could she explain more clearly? But at that moment she was distracted by Wulfie who suddenly heaved himself to his feet and began drinking from the bowl of water that the guard had brought for him.

"Crow, Wulfie's better!" she said. "Look!"

"Don't be so sure," said Crow. "He won't be back to his usual form just yet."

"But we can start to plan!" said Tanith. "How we're going to find Asta and Jed – how we're going to get out of this cell!"

"You think I haven't been doing that already?" said Crow. "The trouble is, I haven't a clue what we can do. I have no idea what my mother is planning; she surely doesn't think I want to stay? And does she really think she can hold me against my will for ever?"

"Ssh!" said Tanith. "I think we may be about to find out – someone's coming."

A guard pulled the curtain aside. He bore a tray loaded with dishes of porridge and honey and a pitcher of milk. A second guard followed, with clothes and towels and a third carrying a bowl and a steaming ewer of hot water.

"Breakfast," said the first. "Be quick. The Pied Piper wants to see you. Then wash and put on these robes. There's soap in the bowl. Be thorough. You stink."

Tanith couldn't suppress a grin. "Charming," she said.

Crow, however, was shaking out the robes suspiciously. "These are very fine," he said. "What's she up to?"

Tanith was busy with the porridge but glanced across and gasped. The soft woollen robes were rich with embroidery and fringed with beaded gemstones.

"Maybe she's trying to win us over?" she said. "Maybe she wants you to be happy to stay?"

"Maybe," said Crow, grimly. "But I wouldn't rely on it."

Once they were clean, dressed and fed, a guard appeared at the door.

"Let's go then," he said. "Follow me."

"What about my dog?" said Tanith. "I'm worried about him."

"He will be taken care of," said the guard.

"He's not fit to move, Tanith," said Crow. "Let him rest."

Tanith knew he was right but looked anxiously over her shoulder. She didn't want to leave Wulfie with the very people who had hurt him.

When they arrived at the Pied Piper's cavern, Tanith and Crow could hear voices – children's voices, refreshingly normal and bright. Tanith clutched Crow's sleeve.

"The kids!" she said. "They sound fine!"

Crow shrugged her off with a frown. She winced at the rebuff but guessed what he was thinking. It wasn't safe for his mother to suspect that they were friends. Tentatively, she followed Crow into the cavern, surprised that the guards were keeping a respectful distance.

Immediately, a cry went up.

"Crow! Crow!"

It was Timbo. At once, the other kids joined in, pushing and jostling to get closer but restrained by a circle of guards. It was obvious, however, that the kids were happy enough – fed, refreshed and clean – and able to think for themselves. But then Timbo raised his voice again.

"Crow," he called out. "Where's Asta? Where's Jed?"

Crow's eyes widened with shock and Tanith, still battered from the previous few days' experiences, felt suddenly dizzy. They had both assumed that Asta and Jed would be with the kids. If not, where were they? They had not noticed Crow's mother when they came in, too absorbed by the sight of the kids, but they heard her now as she laughed and clapped her hands.

"Children, children," she said. "Always something to complain of! Are you not well-fed and clean now? Are you not happy to be safe from that awful city? Is not Crow to be thanked for bringing you all here?"

"But we want Asta," said a little girl in a plaintive voice. "Where's Asta?"

"All in good time, children, I promise," said Crow's mother, smiling. "You must go to your work now. Piper – a tune, please!"

Immediately, an old piper stepped forward, his pipe ready. As soon as the first notes were heard, the kids quietened and followed him docilely from the room.

"There, Crow. You see?" said his mother. "All your little orphans are fed and clothed and ready to do a productive day's work. Are you not happy? Is that not what you wanted?"

"Where are Asta and Jed?" Crow growled. "The kids need them – they need someone they know – just while they're settling in."

The Pied Piper sighed. "Never satisfied, are you, Crow? And don't think you can fool me. The kids need them, indeed. The girl is highly attractive. Don't think I can't guess what your real interest is."

"So?" said Crow. "Where are they?"

His mother sighed again. "Always so demanding, Crow. I see you haven't changed. Where they are – or rather, where they end up – depends on you, Crow. They are old – yes, yes, I know, no older than you but they lack your skills. And it is harder for the old to adapt to our way of life. Oh, we can find jobs for them somewhere, of course, but they aren't a truly useful commodity. Not like the children you have brought.

I would be taking them on as a favour if they stayed."

"But the kids need them," Crow stormed. "They need someone familiar. This is all strange to them."

"They would know you, Crow," said his mother. "If you stayed. And, of course, if I could persuade you to use your mind powers in our service – yes, I know you inherited your father's gift, I'm not entirely stupid – then one favour would be repaying another. But if you choose to leave –" the Pied Piper gazed around the cavern, lips pursed, a little whistle escaping them – "then who knows what might happen?"

"You wouldn't be that cruel!" exclaimed Tanith.

"Silence!" rapped the Pied Piper. "Don't forget that *your* fate isn't sealed yet either. You are only here on sufferance until I decide what to do with you – I have yet to discover the skill that has made you useful to my son, but don't worry, I will find out – and then, perhaps, we too can negotiate. After all, I have your dog. Guard, show her!"

A guard stepped forward and snatched back the curtain draping one of the many entrances. To Tanith's horror, another then dragged Wulfie forth, a rope looped cruelly round his neck. His head was down, his tail between his legs, his eyes still half-closed.

"Wulfie," Tanith cried out, her voice breaking, but the big dog barely lifted his head.

"Stop this, mother," said Crow. "Stop torturing us. You think this makes me want to stay?"

"Want? Want? I don't care what you *want*, Crow. You

have a duty to your people, a precious gift that you could share with them but you have chosen to abandon them and deprive us all of your power, just as your father did. It is what *I* want that matters, I, your Pied Piper, I and the rest of your people. I am still your mother and you are still my child. I want your gifts back and I intend to see that I get them. Bring the others!"

Another rug was pulled back and through it, pushed to their knees in front of the Pied Piper, fell Asta and Jed. Their hands were tied and they were even more dirty and dishevelled than the last time Tanith had seen them. Asta had lost her grubby bandana and her hair tumbled forwards into her pale face which was either very dirty or bruised. Tanith was suddenly horribly aware of the gorgeous robe she was wearing and her fresh, clean body. She and Crow had been trapped.

"Here you are then, my son," said the Pied Piper, her lip curling. "Your friends."

Asta's head shot up, her eyes finding Crow's richly robed figure, her face a mask of shock.

"Your son?" she gasped.

"Oh yes," said the Pied Piper. "Crow is my son. I think his little mission has been quite successful, don't you? A pity he couldn't have found a few more workers for my looms but he's made a good start on this occasion."

"Workers? Mission?" said Asta. "I don't understand."

"Oh, I think you do," said the Pied Piper. "I think it's very clear."

"Asta, it's…" Crow was twisting his hands, his face begging Asta not to believe his mother.

"Save your breath, son," said the Pied Piper. "You don't have to act any more now. Your mission was a success. And remember, nothing is yet decided about your friends."

Crow bit his lip, hoping that Asta would detect the threat in his mother's lying words, hoping she would realize how impossible it was for him to explain – that one word out of place might cost Asta and Jed their lives. But Asta had other concerns.

"So who's she?" she demanded, tossing her head in the direction of Tanith. "Your daughter?"

"I don't know who she is," said the Pied Piper spreading her hands, all transparency. "My son has his own methods. How he used this girl on this particular mission, I have no idea."

"That explains it," cried Asta. "That explains everything!" She turned on Jed. "Don't tell me you're in on this scam too!"

Jed stared at her, lifting his bound hands in appeal. "Does it look like it?" he said.

Tanith wanted to shout at Asta, to tell her not to be taken in, not to trust the Pied Piper, but she could see the guard poised by Wulfie, an unsheathed knife at the ready, hidden from Asta's view. The silent threat made her mute. Crow, however, could no longer stay silent, whatever the risk.

"It isn't true, Asta," he said. "Believe me, you must believe me. This is my mother, that's true, but none of the rest is. I was trying to bring the kids to a safe place, honestly I was."

"So how come you left us? How come you're here now with *her* and you're both dressed up like royalty while we're tied up and starving?"

"I had to find Tanith – you know that! I couldn't leave her to be killed by those hunters or to freeze to death!"

"Is that true?" Asta's tortured eyes were fixed on Tanith in desperation. "You tell me. Is he lying or telling the truth?"

Tanith was watching the bright blade which was up close against Wulfie's throat. If she, Tanith, spoke out now, Wulfie would be killed before her eyes, that was obvious.

So who should she betray? Her dog, her beloved dog, or Crow? And along with Crow, Asta and Jed? The seconds ticked slowly by. The Pied Piper's expression was fixed in a sardonic smile.

"Well?" demanded Asta. "Tell me!"

Tanith's heart was breaking. She couldn't look at Wulfie but he, she knew, would know nothing more if he was to die now. If she didn't tell the truth, however, Asta and Jed would think themselves double-crossed and how would Crow ever forgive her? How would she forgive herself? Her grandmother's story of guilt and remorse would simply have seeded another.

"It's the truth…" she croaked. "Wulfie, forgive me!"

But Crow's reactions, trained by years of city survival, were like lightning. He dived across the space and sent the knife spinning out of the guard's hand, then snatched it up off the floor.

Tanith, expecting Wulfie to die, was suddenly powered by an anger so strong it burned up all her pain. She felt superhuman. The Pied Piper, satisfied that she held all the cards, was complacent. When Tanith lunged for the pipe at her waist and wrenched it from her belt, she was off her guard.

Tanith thrust the little pouch high in the air, backing towards Crow and Wulfie.

"Don't think I won't smash it," she shrieked. "I know it can be done!"

The guards didn't move, waiting for a signal from their mistress. Waiting for her music. She, however, had crumpled, her hands clutching her belt, her face ashen.

"Don't think it can't be replaced!" she said, but her voice was shaking.

Crow had slit the bonds on Asta and Jed.

"Not quickly though," he said. "The making of a pipe is a lengthy art. That's why you broke mine. But now I..." He reached out his hand to take his mother's pipe from Tanith. "Now I have yours. And don't bother to call for another piper. The music has no effect on us. Tanith, here – take this!"

Tanith grabbed the knife he thrust at her and levelled it at the Pied Piper's breast. Her hand was trembling but Wulfie had slunk to her side and was regarding their enemy balefully. Just the knowledge that he had cheated death gave her confidence.

Behind her, Tanith could hear Crow speaking quietly to Asta and then Jed. The talk was a cover, she was sure. He would be meeting their minds and infusing them with resistance to piper music.

"That way," she heard him say. "Go quickly." He ushered his friends though one of the archways, then stepped back into the cavern and spoke quietly to the guards.

"Bind my mother hand and foot," he said, "and take her to the cell where we were housed."

The music Crow played was short and firm. Without hesitation, the guards did as they were bidden.

"Goodbye, Mother," Crow said to the stricken woman who seemed utterly incapable of moving or speaking. Then he beckoned to Tanith and ran.

28

"Crow!" Tanith shouted, hurrying down the winding stairs after him, Wulfie glued to her side. "Crow! Where are you going?"

"I want to find the kids," he hurled over his shoulder. "I need to talk to them. I'll wait at the bottom," he called, disappearing round the bend in the spiral.

Tanith gritted her teeth and struggled to match his speed. Now that the crisis was past, all her superhuman energy had drained away and the aches and pains of the last few days were back with a vengeance. She felt utterly exhausted. It was with grim satisfaction that she reached the bottom of the staircase only seconds after Crow. Asta and Jed were with him.

Minutes later, they were entering the carpet cavern. Crow held up his mother's pipe and waved at a female piper who was at her station on the gallery. She blew a few strident notes and every loom in the cavern was still, the children frozen at their work.

"Crow?" she said, sounding stunned. "Is that you?"

Crow played his signature tune.

The woman still looked wary. "Isn't that your mother's pipe?"

"She is indisposed," said Crow, "and my pipe has been broken. She has sent me to talk with the consignment of children I brought here."

The woman nodded. The explanation seemed to satisfy her. "The children are in the training cave," she said. "You remember where it is?"

Crow nodded and turned aside.

"A moment, Crow," said the woman. He hesitated, clearly uncomfortable. "It is good to see you back," the woman continued. "Gifts such as yours and your father's are always sorely missed."

Crow inclined his head slightly. "I'm sorry," he said, in a low voice. Then he swept out of the cavern, the others hurrying after him.

The training cave had a peaceful air, the music from the trainer's pipe slow and gentle. Tanith felt her whole battered body ease, soothed by the tranquil atmosphere and the repetitive actions of the kids as they learned the basics of weaving. Their scrawny little faces, always so tense and alert, had relaxed. Already the deep shadows beneath their eyes, born of bad nights and tough days, had begun to fade. They looked neat and clean and comfortable, their hair trimmed or tied back, their skin paler for having been well scrubbed. Crow was speaking to the piper, telling his tale of his mother's indisposition. Any moment now the kids would be free to say what they wanted. And that was where the awfulness lay. They could have safety or freedom. But not both. Which, Tanith wondered, would they choose?

Crow told the kids everything, not only about the pipe music but about his own singular gift. Tanith watched Asta's stricken face as she realized how much she had been in Crow's power and felt sick. It was cruel. There should have been time to break the news gently to her on her own. She saw Jed slip his arm protectively around her waist and was glad of it.

"So now you must decide what you want to do," Crow went on. "Return to the city where you risk being butchered or stay here where you will be safe but slaves to the pipe. And I must apologize. I only ever wanted your safety – I never used my powers for anything other than your good – but I wasn't honest. Perhaps I should have been. I'm sorry."

With that, Crow stalked out of the training cavern, his proud face held high, leaving the kids to chatter their astonishment. Tanith struggled to her feet, unsure whether to follow him. She felt a light hand on her shoulder.

"Go on – talk to him," said Asta. "He needs someone he can trust."

"He trusts you," said Tanith.

Asta shook her head. "It's you he wants now. And anyway, right now, I can't…" Asta's strong face crumpled, her lips quivering. "I can't," she said. "I just can't."

"It's all right," said Tanith, clicking her fingers at Wulfie. "I understand. I'll go."

Tanith didn't have far to search. Crow had turned into the nearest staircase lobby and was standing, leaning against the wall, his face sunk into his hands. Tanith had an urge to wrap her arms around his waist and rest her head against his back but had no idea if she would be welcome. Instead she wound her fingers into Wulfie's wiry fur.

"Crow!" she said softly. "Crow!"

He turned wearily.

"Tanith," he said. "What on earth am I going to do?"

Tanith bit her lip. To her the answer seemed obvious but she knew how loathsome it would be to Crow.

"Is there another piper who could lead instead of you or your mother?" she asked.

"I don't know," said Crow. "I was a kid when I left. And we are few. That was one reason my father stayed as long as he did. He knew he would leave a big gap if he went. There might be someone but I have no idea who – and anyway, what's to stop my mother finding support and taking control again? Even if I stayed and tried to rule in her place, she could do that. Most pipers think she does a good job."

Tanith took a deep breath. "Crow, I think they're probably right. I think she probably does." She stepped back, seeking the support of the wall, one hand reaching out to clasp Wulfie's neck.

"What? *What?*" The blast of Crow's fury was at least as powerful as she'd expected. She had, after all, just seen his mother's rage. "Are you *mad*? You met my mother! You saw what she did!"

Tanith's fingers wriggled even deeper into Wulfie's fur and she sidled closer to him for courage. "I told you before," she said. "She's in pain and she's angry. She didn't kill any of us, she didn't even hurt us. We were given the best food I've eaten in years. I'm wearing the most beautiful clothes I've ever had. And the kids, Crow – the kids look *happy*! They're beginning to heal, Crow – already!"

"But at what cost, Tanith? Think of the price they have to pay!"

"I know, I know, Crow! I'm not suggesting that staying here is the perfect solution – it's just the lesser of two evils! If they go back to the city, Crow, they could pay with their *lives*!"

For a long moment, their eyes locked, each determined

to win this battle. But Crow was unused to real confrontation. He was the first to look away.

Tanith spoke slowly, weighing every word. "You told me that your mother wanted to reintroduce lead mining and that was the final straw for your father – right?"

Crow nodded.

"Has she?"

"I haven't seen any evidence," Crow admitted.

"You said that some kids' sight was damaged by the weaving. Does it still happen?"

"How would I know?"

"You could find out. You only have to ask another piper or…"

"Or what?"

"You could talk to your mother."

"Talk to my mother?" Crow stared down at Tanith as if she had taken leave of her senses. "You think I'd believe her?"

"Crow, you could at least give her a chance! It's years since you left. Maybe she's changed. People do, you know! And what were you thinking of doing? Never speaking to her again? Leaving her to rot in a dungeon for ever? Even if you stayed here and became the new Pied Piper, you'd have to talk to her eventually. You can't just pretend she doesn't exist, even if you've successfully managed that for the last few years."

Crow paced up and down the lobby. "I can't stay here," he said, as he swung round, the beaded fringe of his robe fanning out with the force. "I'd go mad, confined to these… these *burrows*! And I despise the way the system works. So I can't be the new piper. Even if I could bear to stay, how could I be the leader here? I have no experience – I wouldn't know where to start!"

"You have no choice, then," said Tanith. "You must talk to your mother."

"I could find my father," said Crow, a gleam of hope in his eye. "He could rule."

"Crow," said Tanith gently, reaching out to him. "Crow, you've been out there for years and you haven't found him yet! You're clutching at straws."

Crow took her hands and bowed his head. "I know," he said. "I know. He could even be dead. It's just…"

They stood for a minute, silent, hands locked. Then Crow stood up straight. "Right," he said. "Right. Let's go and see what the others have decided."

29

When Crow, Tanith and Wulfie returned to the training cavern, everyone fell silent. The piper, Tanith noticed uneasily, had gone.

A knot of kids was clustered around Asta, one small girl huddled on her lap, thumb in mouth. Timbo clung to her side, his eyes anxious.

"Well?" said Crow. "What have you decided?"

Asta's voice was firm. "We want to stay," she said.

Crow flinched. "All of you? You too, Jed?"

"Yes," said Jed. "All of us. There's nothing for us out

there except sickness and death."

"But Jed," said Crow. "It wouldn't be so dangerous for you. Think what you are sacrificing!"

Jed shook his head. "I have done unspeakable things, Crow. In one sense, I came to you too late. If I am to escape my demons, I have to look out for these kids, wherever they go."

"I can't leave them either," said Asta. "You know I can't. It would break their hearts and mine too – and we have all suffered enough heartbreak already. But what will *you* do, Crow?"

At that moment, the training piper burst in through the door, a few armed outsiders at his back.

"Explain yourself, Crow!" he rapped. "I have found our Pied Piper bound hand and foot in a cell which is mind-locked. The guards won't respond to my pipe and let me speak with her. I had my suspicions when you suddenly appeared with your tale of her indisposition – a feeble ruse, I might say, after an absence of five years. If this is a coup, then you can expect opposition. We revere your mother, even if you do not!"

Crow inclined his head politely. "This is no coup," he said. "Be assured of that. There has, I admit, been some difficulty between myself and my mother. My friends and I felt threatened. My mother smashed my pipe. We acted in our own defence. That is all. I will go now to speak with her and attempt to make my peace. If you would care to accompany me, you will see that I intend to return her pipe. I hope it will be acceptable for my friends to wait here until I return?"

The piper looked puzzled but nodded. "It is well," he said. "These men and I will escort you to your mother now. You will come alone?"

Crow looked briefly at Tanith. She nodded.

"Yes," he said. "I will come alone."

Crow's mother had hauled herself to the side of the cell and was sitting against the wall with as much dignity as she could muster. When she saw Crow enter her face froze.

"I had thought," she said, "that you had cut and run."

"With your pipe?" he said. "How would that help the kids I have brought here?"

His mother looked surprised. "You still intend to leave them here?" she said. "As slaves to the pipe? I thought you despised our methods."

"Mother," said Crow. "I brought them to you in the first place, didn't I? Nothing outside here has changed as far as I know." He raised the pipe to his lips and a couple of guards slit his mother's bonds. She shook out her hands, stretched her ankles, and stood up.

"Thank you," she said. "I assume there is still a mind-lock on the door."

Crow smiled ruefully. "I'm afraid so," he said. "You smashed my pipe, mother. I don't want to take foolish risks but I would rather you were comfortable."

"So," said his mother. "City living has not made you entirely ungracious."

"I have never forgotten our ways," said Crow. He blinked rapidly. A wave of nostalgia was washing over him. His last years in the caves had been soured by the acrimony between his parents but now he remembered the good times – the hours on the wind-swept hills, the velvety softness of his fine-spun clothes, the wholesome satisfaction of a well-cooked meal and his mother, young, blonde and beautiful, remote for the most part but ever patient as she supervised his daily pipe practice. He had been desperate to avoid her displeasure, worshipping her from a distance.

The silence between them grew and Crow did not know how to break it.

"Crow," said his mother, at last. "Crow, I behaved very badly earlier."

Crow stared at her, incredulous.

She shook her head, smiling. "Oh Crow," she said. "You never did see the real me, did you? You always saw the Pied Piper – or the witch your father depicted." Here her voice grew bitter.

"Not a *witch*," said Crow.

His mother shrugged. "I don't know, Crow. I don't know what he said to you. I just know that while I was busy trying to rule, he was the one who had your ear – and when things began to go wrong between us, you only really heard his side. I'm not blaming him. I just wish it could have been different. He was right about many things – but he was such a hothead. He wanted to destroy the way we work –

but he had no plans for our survival or for the outsiders. Were they just to be thrust out into the world with no work, no homes, no means to live? We know only too well what it's like out there. You know too now – and you have chosen to bring your little band of children back to us."

"The lead mining," said Crow, his voice shaking. "Were you going to reintroduce that?"

"I considered it," said his mother. "I considered it for a long time. But your father convinced me it would be wrong. The work would be too harsh – too dangerous. But he left before he knew that. It was my fault. We rowed about it and I was too proud to let him see that he had won or to send anyone after him. I paid for it when you left. You are so like your father, Crow. Strong, determined, compassionate, caring – but a rebel and a hothead. I should have realized that you would follow him – but I was blinded by bitterness and jealousy."

"Jealousy?"

"Yes. He left me for a world of disease and danger. How do you think that made me feel?"

"But I thought…I thought your marriage was arranged! I thought it was all about producing a child who combined your gifts!"

"Yes, it was – but that didn't mean we didn't love each other. We did – passionately. But we were complete opposites – so in the end, we clashed – and we did that passionately as well. Too passionately for your father, it would seem."

"I never knew," said Crow.

"How could you?" said his mother. "I was never close to you. I was always the Pied Piper. Since you both left, I have worked hard to make this place as comfortable as possible for the outsiders. No child ever loses their eyesight on the looms, no weakness or injury is ever overlooked. If your father returned he would still accuse me of keeping slaves and he is right, I do. But I know how it is outside and I cannot think what alternative there is. We are trapped – every single one of us."

"Why didn't you tell me all this?" said Crow. "Why did you smash my pipe and try to blackmail me?"

Crow's mother smiled grimly. "Blame my pride," she said. "If you returned, I wanted you to be impressed. So when you thrust that bunch of mangy, filthy kids in at our doors and then disappeared without so much as a greeting, I was beside myself. I had longed for you to return for five years and when you came, it was as if you had spat in my face."

"I'm sorry," said Crow. "I should have stayed. I would have done. But I had left Tanith on the hillside. Hunters were threatening her. I had to go back and find her. She could have been killed."

"Tanith? The girl with the dog?"

"Yes."

"You are fond of her? What about the other girl? The tall, striking one?"

"Asta."

"What about her? She watches your every move."

Crow sighed. "It's difficult," he said. "Asta has been my friend and helper for three years. I...I..."

"She loves you but you don't love her?"

"I don't know. I...the thing is, Tanith is special. My mind powers have no effect on her. I couldn't *make* her like me if I tried. But Asta..."

Crow's mother smiled. "It doesn't matter how it happened, my son," she said. "The tall girl loves you. You can be sure of that."

"She wants to stay here," said Crow. "So she must love the kids more."

"We all have our burdens, Crow. And sometimes they stand in the way of what we really want. I myself know that only too well."

"You mean...?"

"I mean that I didn't choose to be Pied Piper of this place. But that is my role in this world and I must live it."

There was a difficult silence. Crow found that he couldn't meet his mother's eyes. She sighed.

"You are determined to go then? To deprive us of your gifts? To deprive me again of my son?"

"I'm sorry, Mother. I *can't* stay," said Crow. "It's not just the system here – it's the caves themselves. I hate being confined. I'm sure I'd go mad before long."

"You wouldn't need to be confined. You could choose what work you wanted. An ambassador, a courier, a farmer – any such role might suit you."

Crow shook his head. "Perhaps one day," he said. "But the truth is, I have to know what happened to my father."

His mother inclined her head. "Then I must hope that you find him quickly," she said.

Crow untied the pipe pouch which he had fastened to his belt.

"I need to return this," he said, holding it out. "In just a few hours, the kids look happier than they have all the time I have cared for them. I should have brought them long ago."

"No," said his mother. "You have done your best for them, Crow, I am sure." She got to her feet and took the pipe.

"Well then…" said Crow, awkwardly. "It's time for me to go."

"Without your pipe?" said his mother. "Surely you would be wise to wait for us to fashion you a new one?"

Crow shook his head. "No," he said. "It is not the way I want to live. I cannot choose to leave behind my mind power – but I choose to leave my pipe. Pipe work has been responsible for much evil."

"And great good," said his mother. "You yourself have shown that."

"No," said Crow. "It is a two-edged tool in my hands and I fear its temptations. I would rather go at once."

"As you will," said his mother but for the first time, her voice shook. She took a step towards Crow. "I wish I could persuade you to stay," she said and for a moment Crow thought he could detect a sob in her voice. "But believe me, I am very proud that you won't give in. That girl, Tanith – I hope she appreciates what she has found."

Crow could barely speak for the pain in his throat but he tried anyway.

"Asta," he croaked. "You will take care of Asta, won't you, Mother?"

"I promise, my son," she said. "You can trust me, I promise."

30

Tanith blinked and forced her eyes open again. The kids were back at the training looms. Asta and Jed were slumped against each other, fast asleep, and Wulfie lay curled up beside Tanith, snoring. Tanith, however, had seated herself upright against the wall, her short legs crossed uncomfortably, determined to be awake when Crow returned. Even so and despite her anxiety, her head kept lolling. She longed to give in to the heavy wooziness that had invaded her whole body but although she guessed it was only a reaction to days of tension, she couldn't be sure. Better to stay awake in this strange place of pipe music and mind power.

Suddenly, brisk footsteps approached the cave. Many footsteps. Tanith hauled herself up, rubbed her eyes and pulled aside the rug which shrouded the entrance.

"Crow!" she said and then, seeing his mother, "Your ...er...your Majesty."

The Pied Piper, flanked by her guards, nodded but stood back. Crow hurried forwards and clasped Tanith's hands.

"You were right," he said.

Tanith searched his face anxiously. "Are you okay?" she asked.

"Yes," he said. "I'm all right now. But I'm still going to leave. I'm still going to try to find my father."

"Yes, I know," said Tanith. "It's something you have to do. Like I had to find out what happened to the kids in my grandmother's story. And I have. It was bad but it's better now. So I'm free."

"So what will you do now?" Crow's piercing dark eyes were fixed on hers.

Tanith returned his gaze, utterly unclouded.

"Come with you, of course," she said. "If you want me to."

"Of course I want you to," said Crow and, holding her gently, he kissed her.

*

It was a large group that accompanied Tanith and Crow to the entrance gate, once they had been kitted out with robust clothes and basic provisions. Others who remembered Crow, both pipers and outsiders, had come to see him off. Much to his discomfort, several had begged him to stay but he had remained resolute.

"I have to go," he insisted. "This is not the place for me and I need to find my father."

"Perhaps when you have, you will be more comfortable here," said the training piper.

"Perhaps," said Crow, "but I cannot know that until I have tried."

The kids, despite their obvious relish for their new life, were subdued. Timbo, red-eyed and snivelling clung to Asta's arm. When they reached the gate, Crow turned to everyone.

"This is where we must part," he said, firmly. "Kids, you have a new life here. Make the most of it."

"I want to come with you to the outside," sobbed Timbo. "I want to wave goodbye."

Crow crouched down and put his hands on the little boy's shoulders. "Wave goodbye from here, Tim," he said. "Stay inside where you know you're safe."

Crow's mother stepped forward and put a hand on Timbo's shoulder.

"Be brave, young man," she said. "Just because you have left the city, does not mean you can abandon your courage."

Timbo gulped and sniffed valiantly.

"All right," he said. "G...goodbye, Crow. And thank you for saving my life." He turned round to find Asta but she had stepped outside the gates.

"Jed's just there, Timbo," she called, nodding in Jed's direction. "I'll be back in a few minutes, I promise."

In silence, Crow, Asta, Tanith and Wulfie walked up the tunnel. The slit of light at the end gradually grew bigger and brighter. Tanith found herself blinking; she had become so used to the dimmer light of the sconces.

"We can walk straight out?" she asked.

"We can," said Crow, "but Asta mustn't. She wouldn't be able to get back in without me."

"So this is goodbye then," said Asta.

Tentatively, Tanith held out her arms and Asta stepped into them. They hugged quickly.

"Goodbye, Asta," said Tanith. "I think you are the strongest, kindest girl I've ever met – though I didn't think so at first!"

"And you're the toughest and the bravest," said Asta. "Take care, okay?" Then she took Wulfie's big head in her hands and fondled his ears. "Goodbye, Wulfie," she said. "Look after my friends."

Wulfie whined but had half an eye on the rolling moorland outside.

"I'm sorry," said Tanith, laughing. "He's thinking 'rabbits', I'm afraid. Come on, Wulfie. We'll wait for you just down the hill, Crow."

Crow and Asta watched Tanith hobble down the slope after Wulfie, who had bounded off the moment his nose sniffed fresh air.

"She's amazing," said Asta.

"So are you," said Crow. Gently, he wiped away her tears with his thumb. "You could still come with us, you know," he whispered, choked.

"No." Asta shook her head. "You know that wouldn't work. She's what you want and need. And the kids need me. Besides, do you really think I want to be with someone who can manipulate my mind with a glance? However much I love him?"

"I'm so sorry, Asta," said Crow. "Can you ever forgive me?"

Asta tossed back her gleaming dark curls and smiled wryly. "I'm working on it," she said. Then she reached up, took Crow's face in her hands and kissed him.

"There," she said. "My choice, all right?"

For a moment, Crow rested his forehead against hers. "And mine," he said. Then he kissed her goodbye.

Tanith was waiting in the crook of one of the gnarled boulders which studded the hillside while Wulfie gambolled about, as excited as a puppy. She noted Crow's frown and the sharp, tight set of his lips.

"Sure about this?" she said quietly.

Crow cast one quick glance back up the hill then turned his face into the brisk, wintry wind. He adjusted his pack and his firestaff and held out his hand to Tanith.

"Sure," he said. And they set off in the direction of the city.

MEG HARPER is the successful author of several children's series and her first novel, *Fur*, was shortlisted for the Highland Children's Book Awards 2007. As well as being a busy writer and mum, Meg teaches youth theatre, and is a member of three book groups, including one for children, and a film group. She loves swimming and walking – especially if the walk ends at a tea shop!

Meg lives in Warwickshire with her husband, four teenagers, a cat and two chickens. To find out more about Meg Harper, you can visit her website: www.megharper.co.uk

In this story, choices that no one should ever have to make, are made. Many children living today have no choice. They are enslaved.

Visit www.stopthetraffik.org

Meg Harper

fur

by Meg Harper

**Shortlisted for the Highland Children's
Book Awards 2007**

Grace loves swimming in the sea; it soothes her when she's restless and comforts her when she's sad. Even her dreams are full of the scents and sounds of the ocean.

But dark shadows are troubling the peaceful waters of Grace's life. Her body is beginning to change, but not as she expected. And now that she's started seeing Nik, will she be able to keep her secret to herself?

"A poignant story of first love that teenage girls especially will enjoy, with its added element of fantasy."   Write Away!

"Meg Harper's wonderful story of how Grace discovers the story of her ancestry entrances the reader every step of the way, with twists and turns and an unexpected ending... a truly gripping summer read."   The Glasgow Herald

£5.99
ISBN 9780746073056

For more mysterious and compelling tales
check out
www.fiction.usborne.co.uk